With Love to Yourself and Baby

by

John R. Alstadt Jr.

John R. Alstadt, Jr.

DORRANCE PUBLISHING CO., INC.
PITTSBURGH, PENNSYLVANIA 15222

ISBN # 0-8059-5251-9
Printed in the United States of America

First Printing

For information or to order additional books, please write:
Dorrance Publishing Co., Inc.
643 Smithfield Street
Pittsburgh, Pennsylvania 15222
U.S.A
1-800-788-7654
Or visit our web site and on-line catalog at
www.dorrancepublishing.com

Dedication

To my mother, Alice Jean (Brown) Alstadt,
with my deepest gratitude and admiration.

The Dover Tragedy

No more terrible tragedy was ever known in Delaware than the poisoning case in Dover. . . . No crime could be more detestable and none should appeal more powerfully to every agony designed for the protection of society.

Delaware Gazette and State Journal
August 18, 1898

Contents

Author's Foreword and Acknowledgments

Our story begins, as many do, with a single scrap of information gleaned from notebooks long forgotten. In 1992, the author was serving on the board of directors for Dover Heritage Trail, a local historic group, when he chanced to find an old newspaper clipping. The short story was entitled "Old Timers Recall Famed Poison Candy Case That Stirred Delaware Back in the '90s."

A veteran police officer having served with the *Delaware State Police* for eighteen years, the author's interest was peaked. As a full-time criminalist in the homicide unit and also a student working on his master's degree in history, he was forced to place the story in his memory banks. At the time, there was little extra time for any other endeavor. He vowed that in the near future he would learn the whole truth of the events which were recounted.

Six years later the moment arrived. The author was compiling information for a new endeavor which was about to reach fruition. He had retired from police work and was pursuing his second love in life, historical research. The results of this research led to the development of "Shadows of the Past: The Walking Tour of Old Dover." The tour placed him in close proximity to the location where "The Poison Candy Murder Case" had happened one hundred years prior.

His interest peaked, the author was spurred on a quest to find all the factual evidence which existed pertaining to this infamous crime. Solving the mystery involved travel throughout the State of Delaware to research facilities. It also meant that transcontinental travel would have to be undertaken to the San Francisco Bay area to research establishments there. Why, one may ask? The answer is that this case was the "first murder by mail" in the United States.

In Delaware, where the victims resided, the information left to posterity centered on newspaper accounts and miniscule documentation filed in the Delaware State Archives. The travel to San Francisco was necessitated by the fact that this is where the defendant resided and where the trials took place. Unfortunately information here also relied mostly on the numerous newspapers of the era. One book, *San Francisco Murders,* did exist which offered a short chapter pertaining to the case, but it was based largely on newspaper accounts.

The hunt for additional factual information seemed fruitless due to an event which occurred April 18, 1906, and is known to history as the San Francisco earthquake and fire. It appeared that all the evidence and documentation relating to the case had been destroyed. The trail was fast coming to a dead end regarding supportive evidence to the multitude of newspaper clippings. At this time, the author contacted the State of California Archives in Sacramento, on the slim chance that some bit of information had been deposited within their vaults.

Given the blind alleys so far encountered, the chances for a positive response were minimal at best. It was difficult to contain the excitement within, when the researcher, after being given the name "Cordelia Botkin," stated, "We have the entire transcript and appeals." With this information securely in hand, the final chapter of the *Infamous Poison Candy Murder Case* was about to be written. The quest, which had its minuscule beginnings some eight years earlier, was coming full circle.

At this point I would like to thank those wonderful people who have supported me in this endeavor. To Elisa, I say thank you, for your support, assistance with research, and artistic ability; to my friend and typist, Marla Carter, who aided me in time and spirit and for the never-ending hours of proofreading and subtle corrections, thank you; to Gene Grace, friend and scholar, thank you for your grammatical wisdom; to my mother, who infused me with the desire to solve a good mystery, thank you.

I acknowledge those individuals and research staffs without whose assistance the present work would be but an unfulfilled dream. The San Francisco History Center especially Patricia Akre, photographic curator; the staff of the State of California Archives; the University of Delaware; the City of San Francisco Museum; the Ansel Adams Photographic Center; the Historical Society of Delaware; Sandra Harris, California Researcher; and Delaware State Archives with a special thanks to James Frazier and Karen Donovan.

With this said, I present this book to the memory of John B. Pennington and to his daughters who suffered a tragic death so long ago and whose story is now told.

Introduction

This is a tale of murder most foul where the protagonist never saw the victims. For that matter, she was so far removed from the scene that the heinous deed made little or no sense to the common man. It is said that this "modem day Lucretia Borgia" placed the non-descript package in the United States Mail and thus became the first person in history to "murder by mail."

It is a tale so morbid and vulgar to the Victorian Age, which was an era of romantic deeds and promoted love and nature, as to bring fear to the hearts of those who remembered it. The murders were so base that it gives new meaning to the "Gilded Age," where times were light and pleasurable, free and pure, and good times ran rampant.

The Victorian Age, which lasted the greater part of the nineteenth century (1837-1901), saw some of the most significant advances in technology and invention. Certainly there were political and social themes underlying the time, but this was also the period of the great poets and novelists. Murder was, assuredly, not unknown, but it was confined to specific reasons taking the form of domestic related murders or ones which encompassed economic gains. As the century progressed, however, there seemed to be a darker side which was evolving. Random murder began to set a precedent and come to the forefront, but it was more a dominion of males, not the gentile female, as evidenced by Theodore Durrant, Albert Hoff, Neil Cream and, the infamous Whitechapel murderer, Jack the Ripper.

The murderess was an oddity in this age, though she did exist. It was an age of disbelief that women could for the sake of crime, murder. Lizabeth (Lizzie) Borden was one who comes to mind, but then she was acquitted. Florence Maybrick in England was convicted of murder by arsenic but was later released. Both of these cases, as well as the case of Martha Bowers, occurred within the same decade as did the Poison Candy case. Yes, Lizzie was accused of two hatchet murders, but recall if you will, she first attempted to buy prussic acid to clean sealskin.

Another strange coincidence concerning our present account is the fact that Lucretia Borgia and Cordelia Botkin both contain fourteen letters. Is there a meaning to this? Probably not, but it is food for thought. Consider this also: on August 4, 1892, Andrew and Abby Borden, the parents of Lizzie, were slain with an axe. Cordelia Botkin placed a mysterious package in the mail from San Francisco, August 4, 1898. Similarities between these cases abound, though there are a number of differences.

It is unfortunate that many of the details of this infamous case and the subsequent trials have been lost to posterity. The San Francisco Earthquake and Fire, April 18, 1906, did what Cordelia Botkin was unable to do and virtually erased the memory of this terrible crime and by the merest chance of fate, almost propelled the murderess to martyrdom in one of earth's greatest calamities.

On that fateful day the ground trembled and the walls of the Branch County Jail shook and then began to fall. Cordelia Botkin, twice convicted of the death of Mary Elizabeth Dunning, had avoided the death penalty and was serving a life sentence. While hundreds perished, death took a holiday, and Cordelia and her fellow prisoners were spared to live another day.

To her death, Cordelia maintained her innocence though the State of California put forth a compelling circumstantial case proving her guilt beyond reasonable doubt. Thus herein is presented the factual account of the case, which is a tale of two cities a continent apart sharing, for a time in 1898 a common thread.

Chapter One

Sweet, Virtuous: She Had Few Suspicions of Her Fellow Man

Mary Elizabeth Dunning was an extremely pious woman who had a very high sense of morality. She had married John P. Dunning, February 12, 1891, in the Old Presbyterian Church at Meeting House Square in Dover, Delaware. Shortly after the wedding, the couple had moved to San Francisco where Mr. Dunning had taken a position as the manager of the Associated Press Office.

Subsequent events would show that they lived together from 1891 to 1896 in a relationship which had only the slightest modicum of decorum. As events unfolded later, it was apparent that Mary Elizabeth had been forced to endure years of neglect and continual philandering by her husband. For reasons known only to Mary she chose in 1896 to traverse the continent and return to Dover to live with her parents, three thousand miles from the man she had married.

Returning home to the place of her birth appears to have been a godsend to Mary, for it seemed to bring her an inner peace. Here she would remain, with her baby daughter, Mary Elizabeth (her namesake), far from the glitter and verbose atmosphere of San Francisco. She spoke little of those days in the not so distant past, but instead she basked in the closeness of kinship and friends while enjoying the small town setting.

Dover, Delaware, by any standard, was a small town in the 1890s. With a population explosion in the third quarter of the nineteenth century, its population has risen dramatically. This quaint town of three thousand souls had the distinction of being planned and laid out by William Penn in 1717. It was only recently that its character had changed with the addition of Bradford City and Fulton's Addition, which tripled its size.

To the casual observer of the day, the Public Square was plain in nature, an unadorned square. On its margins were a number of substantial homes occupied by the town's more affluent residents. There were interspersed also a few law firms of import, two banking houses, a hotel, and several public buildings occupied by both the county and the state.

Not particularly attractive in appearance, it was the nerve center of this small, unobtrusive community. It had been left to nature's care without the usual statuary or commemorative monuments to the heroes of a bygone age. Interesting to a small degree, the Public Square to a stranger was therefore not imposing and the visitor would have no inkling of the comedies and tragedies which had occurred on this site. Dover was, in all respects, the complete opposite of a city like San Francisco with its vast size and population.

The Victorian Age had spawned new and ornate architecture, but it only recently had reached Delaware and its capital city. This, then, was the town to which Mary Elizabeth returned. It was a town where she found safety and security. A sigh of relief surely must have pursed her lips as she alighted from the train at the foot of Loockerman Street.

With little fanfare, she and little Mary made their way to the home of her father, The Honorable John B. Pennington, lawyer and statesman. The home which he had leased, was a fine colonial purported to contain forty rooms. Scenically placed in the northwest corner of the Public Square (The Green), number 20, known locally as the Saulsbury Mansion. Built circa 1792 by the Miller family, it was one of the more impressive homes on the square.

Residing within were John Pennington and his wife Rebecca Rowan Pennington; his eldest daughter, Ida Henrietta; her husband, Joshua D. Deane; and their daughter, Leila. A grandson Harry (Henry) Pennington, who lived with an uncle, Dr. George R. Carmicheal, in Wilmington but spent summers with "Grandpa," was also in residence. A colored handyman/servant and Rosy, the colored cook, completed the household. Thus, Mary Elizabeth came home to the city which was the antithesis of San Francisco.

On the horizon, however, events were taking shape which would shock and perplex the citizens of this tiny hamlet. Dover, in stark contrast to the worldliness and glitter of that City by the Bay a continent away, was quiet, complacent, and relatively crime free. It is not to say that crime nor criminals were unknown, but they certainly were not the norm.

Old timers could count on their fingers events which were truly newsworthy. There was the time back in the 1880s when a Philadelphia millionaire, J. Edward Addicks, attempted to bribe Delaware politicians into electing him to the United States Senate. Known nationally as the "Addicks Affair," it had vaulted Dover to nationwide prominence.

Then, too, they remembered back in 1883 the fight between a local man and a circus worker which, some say, led to much rowdiness. Several of the local man's compatriots "shot up" the circus wagons as they passed through town. Neither of these events was really of any magnitude, but murder most foul was, and especially in Dover, it was an anomaly.

There was one murder of a horrendous nature, but that was in '72, eons ago. As the story went Dr. Isaac West, who was not really a doctor, had murdered a colored handyman, Cooch Turner. West thought he could pass the dead man off for himself and collect on a large insurance policy. The ghastly circumstances surrounding this murder paled, however, in comparison to the decadent crime, which loomed on the horizon.

The double tragedy which was about to take place would vault Dover, Delaware, once again into national prominence, and it would remain there for the next decade. The dog days of August 1898 were upon Dover, and soon too would be the stench of death.

Chapter Two

Poisoning Case at Dover: The Mysterious Package

On Tuesday, August 9, 1898, Dover was under the ever-oppressive heat and humidity of the weather which was characteristic for this time of the year. Though not exceedingly hot, the temperatures ranged from the mid sixties to high seventies. Intermittent showers, which were always prevalent in the month of August, had plagued the community. The day had been like any other in the summer for young Harry Pennington. The times he spent with his beloved grandfather away from the hustle and bustle of Wilmington, fifty miles to the north, were dear to him.

As one of his daily chores after supper, as they called the evening meal in Dover, Harry had made the short trek to the post office two blocks north at Loockerman Street and Main Street. Home postal delivery was unknown in this age and each family had a specific box within the post office. His grandfather's was P. 0. Box 335, and the dutiful grandson, after sharing the appropriate pleasantries with the staff, retrieved the mail from within. It included a number of pieces of personal correspondence this day as well as a box for his Aunt Mary Elizabeth. Formal in nature, the plain manila paper correspondence was addressed to "Mrs. John P. Dunning, Dover, Deleware."

As he made the return trip to his grandfather's residence he remarked to himself that the sender of the package had indeed been remiss, it was obvious that geography was not this person's forte in life. "Delewere" should, as all knew, have been spelled Delaware. All who lived in Delaware knew the proper spelling, and he mused in his mind concerning from whence it had originated.

Arriving home, he was met by the usual entourage on the veranda of Grandpa's spacious home and immediately dispensed with the perplexing thought regarding the sender. His grandfather, as was his daily practice, had reclined in the parlor for a nap, and his Uncle Joshua had returned to his shop on Loockerman Street to complete the day. On the veranda that night was his grandmother Rebecca, his aunts Mary Elizabeth and Ida Henrietta, and his cousins Mary E. (Dunning) and Leila (Deane).

Having passed the package to Aunt Elizabeth, he and the others waited in eager anticipation to view the contents. After remarking about the package and its unknown sender, Mary Elizabeth removed the wrapper. Inside she found an assortment of chocolates, a pretty lace handkerchief, and a note: "With love to yourself and baby, Mrs. C."

"Mrs. C." she mused must be her friend, Mrs. Laura Corbaley (Cordaley) 1037 Ellis Street, San Francisco; she had always been so thoughtful. As the wrapper was passed to those present on the veranda all were in agreement regarding the postmark, though indistinct; it read SAN FRAN. . . . The box marked decoratively BON BONS and tied with pretty ribbons was then passed amongst the occupants of the veranda. Coinciding with this, Mr. Pennington had risen from his nap and exited the house. Elizabeth said to him, "Look Papa, someone has sent me a present, but I do not know who it is from!" He declined the offered chocolates, and after exchanging pleasantries, made his way to his office across the Public Square.

Those remaining sampled the confections which did not seem to have faired well on the journey. Mrs. Pennington spat hers out immediately and remarked that she did not think it was very good chocolate. Mrs. Dunning and Mrs. Deane ate heartily of the chocolates, and the children were each given a small sample. Two others who ate of the chocolates were Ethel Millington, daughter of George Millington proprietor of the Capital Hotel, and Josephine Bateman, a local schoolteacher. Out for an evening stroll with Ethel Clarke, they had stopped to exchange pleasantries.

That night after all had retired Mary Elizabeth, Ida Henrietta, Harry, Leila, Ethel Millington, and Josephine Bateman all became ill in varying degrees. Each suffered from vomiting, purging, fever, and headaches through the next days. Mary Elizabeth and Ida Henrietta suffered in the extreme, while the rest were ill to a lesser degree. No one was suspicious at this point, and the cause was laid to cholera morbus (food poisoning), a common ailment of the time.

The illness progressed on August 10 and worsened to such an extent that greatly alarmed, Joshua Deane sent for the family physician, Dr. L. A. H. Bishop who lived next door at number 16 Public Square. Examining Mary and Ida, he ministered to each using the common medicants of the day. The illness progressed, however, and as it worsened, Dr. Bishop consulted with a second physician, Dr. Presley Downes. Both agreed that the course of action taken by Dr. Bishop was correct at the moment, and the prescribed medications were continued.

On August 11 at 4:30 P.M., Mrs. Deane, her condition worsening and in extreme pain, convulsed one last time and died. Her sister, Mary Elizabeth lingered on for thirty hours more. She too finally succumbed to the disorder on August 12 at 8:45 P.M. The children and the neighbors who had also partaken of the sweets convalesced through the weekend and recovered.

John B. Pennington, filled with grief after the loss of his two healthy, vibrant daughters, was left to contemplate the circumstances. He recalled the mysterious package, which arrived that fateful night, August 9. Shortly before Mary's death he had asked her of its location. Between spasms of pain, Mary had related that it was on top of the secretary in the downstairs parlor. Shortly before her death, he had retrieved the wrapper, the box, and its contents.

Following the deaths, he made a cursory examination. There was a familiarity to the writing on the brown paper wrapper. Taking the wrapper with him he walked briskly to his office in the Old County Building at the northeast corner of Public Square. From his desk he retrieved the envelopes of two anonymous letters that Mary Elizabeth had received in the summer of 1897. There was a strong similarity between all the handwriting, but more important was the fact that all contained the same postmark, SAN FRANCISCO.

His suspicions were aroused, but any investigation would have to wait. The more pressing matter at hand was the burial of his last two children. Mr. and Mrs. Pennington were now childless. A son, Harry, and a daughter, Clara had predeceased Mary and Ida. The weekend would be spent in preparation and mourning for the two so recently departed.

The bodies of the two sisters were placed in the care of Undertaker Pritchett who embalmed them. They were then placed side by side in the family parlor, each in a handsome black cloth casket, amidst a multitude of flower arrangements received from the community. On the lids of the caskets the inscription read:

IDA H. DEANE.
DIED AUGUST 11, 1898
AGED 44 YEARS

MARY ELIZABETH DUNNING
DIED AUGUST 12, 1898
AGED 35 YEARS

August 15, 1898, was a day of mourning for the people of Dover. The ancient bell in the tower of the Old Presbyterian Church, where both ladies were members, tolled its mournful sound. Nearly three thousand mourners passed into and exited from the parlor of the Pennington house to express their sorrow. After church services conducted by the Reverend Joseph Brown Turner and Reverend J. F. Stonecipher later in the day, the two sisters were laid to rest head to head sharing a common stone in the *Old Presbyterian Cemetery*.

The task at hand completed by John B. Pennington, former attorney general for the State of Delaware, set the wheels in motion for the apprehension of the murderer or murderess of his darling daughters. Telegrams were sent to Mary Elizabeth's husband, John P. Dunning, requesting that he respond home immediately. Mr. Dunning was now a correspondent with the Associated Press and, at the moment, was in Puerto Rico reporting on the events of the Spanish-American War. He was notified simply that Mary Elizabeth had died and that it was the desire of family to have him home to share in their grief. Beyond this there was no hint of the fate which had befallen his wife nor was there any mention of the death of his sister-in-law.

As John Pennington awaited Dunning's return, he consulted with Dr. Bishop who, after being apprised of the candy, was now of the opinion that the two women may have died of something other than natural causes. Dr. Bishop with this additional knowledge requested some of the pieces that he might take them to the Delaware College in Newark for analysis. Four to five pieces were given to him by Mr. Pennington, and he set forth immediately by train to the college.

At Delaware College, Dr. Bishop consulted with Theodore Wolfe, professor of chemistry. From Wolfe he requested an immediate analysis of the chocolates for arsenic specifically. By the late afternoon, Dr. Wolfe had completed the required testing and entrained to Dover where the inquest into the deaths of Mary Elizabeth and Ida Henrietta was being held.

Prior to the funeral, on August 15, Mr. Pennington had conferred with Coroner William Walls and requested the empanelling of a jury at the prothonotary's office in the courthouse. Even in his grief, the venerable old gentleman, John B. Pennington, was a force with which to be reckoned. The jury consisting of fourteen Doverites had viewed the bodies prior to burial and then went immediately into session. The jury was composed of the following: John B. Collins, C. S. Pennewell, Stephen Slaughter, L. M. Wright, Daniel Cowgill, John Carrow, E. L. Clark, T. J. Stevenson, Walter Morris, John W. Casson, William M. Hazel, W. T. Hutson, James Virdin, and J. Frank Wild.

They were shown the mysterious package and its contents during the course of the proceedings. The package was made of pasteboard measuring 7¼ inch by 3¼ inch and 1¾ inch deep. It was wrapped in common manila paper and contained chocolates with a sprinkling of other candies. The address on the wrapper was clear: "Mrs. John P. Dunning Dover, Delewere." As for the postmark, it was somewhat obscured but was readable. It stated "SAN FRAN. . . . The date of mailing was "AUG. . . ." In addition to the candy also contained in the box were a small handkerchief and a short note (torn from a larger piece of paper), "With love to yourself and baby . . . Mrs. C." (*Delaware Gazette and State Journal*, August 16, 1898).

In addition, to the evidence described, the jury heard testimony from Dr. Lemuel A. H. Bishop, Dr. Presley Downes, and Professor Theodore Wolfe. At the conclusion of the Coroner's Inquest on August 16, 1898, the jury went into deliberation and within a short time returned with a verdict indicating that the deaths had been caused by poisoned candy placed there by a person or persons unknown. The official cause of death, which appeared on the death certificates as signed by William Walls August 17, 1898, was "Arsenic Poison sent by U.S. Mail by parties unknown."

Mr. Pennington, at the conclusion of the inquest issued the following public statement to the *Delaware Gazette and State Journal*, August 17, 1898:

I have no doubt that the package came from San Francisco. The postmark shows it and I have other reasons for so believing. This is not an ordinary case like where one man kills another and you start a hue and cry and go after him. This is a case, which will require hard and quiet work.

Chapter Three

Poisoning Still a Mystery: A Dastardly Plot Suspected

Within hours of John Pennington's brief statement, the State of Delaware began to muster its resources and set in motion the initial aspects of the investigation which was channeled to apprehend the person or persons responsible for this fiendish act. On the 17th of August, Mr. Pennington met with the two state detectives assigned to the case. At this time he made available to Bernard McVey and Walter Witsik the initial evidence which had been collected and was in his possession. Based on this, McVey returned to Wilmington and began the task of determining the manufacturer and location from which the deadly package had come.

Bernard J. McVey had a well-deserved reputation within the state for his ability to ferret clues from the obscure. On this day he added to those laurels by tracing the box itself through Wilmington, Delaware, to Philadelphia, Pennsylvania. The makers of the box added a vital clue to the case. When asked if they had any customers of their boxes in San Francisco, the makers responded only one, the George Haas Candy Company. Within hours instead of days or weeks, Detective McVey had broken the case.

This new information, as well as the candy wrapper, and the anonymous letters in Mr. Pennington's possession gave the case its direction and it was only necessary to speak with John P. Dunning to confirm the growing suspicions. It would be two more days until his arrival from Puerto Rico, but the wheels of justice did not stop.

On the 18th, Governor Ebe Tunnell issued the following notice as an inducement for information resulting in the ultimate capture of the persons responsible for the crime. Posters were printed posthaste and sent to the four corners of the nation and read as follows:

> The Governor's Proclamation:
> Reward: A record of $2,000.00 will be paid by the State of Delaware for the arrest and conviction of the person or persons who caused the death of Mrs. Ida H. Deane and Mrs. Mary Elizabeth Dunning, of the town of Dover, on the 11th and 12th days of August, 1898, by poisoning, through the means of a box of candy sent through the mails.
>
> August 18, 1898
> Ebe W. Tunnell
> Governor

As the proclamation by the Governor went to print, he closeted himself with Attorney-General Robert White, Mr. Pennington, and attorney Edward Ridgley. Their conversations were kept confidential but at their conclusion the Governor made the following statement:

> This is the most horrible crime that has ever occurred in our State. It was a brutal, terrible crime. The person who sent the box of poison candy is as bad, yes, is worse, than the miserable anarchist who throws a bomb into a crowd of innocent and unsuspecting people. The reward which I have offered is the largest ever offered in Delaware, I believe, but the gravity of the case demands it. I hope that the reward is large enough to create an interest in the case and to induce officers and detectives to give their time and attention to it in order to capture the murderer. I hope that this mystery will be unraveled and the guilty person brought to the punishment deserved. The details of the case and its investigation are in the hands of the attorney-general. With that I have nothing to do and shall refer everyone to him, but I am sure that everything possible will be done to place the guilt of the crime. *Every Evening*, August 19, 1898.

At the conclusion of the day, Attorney-General White returned to Wilmington to consult with his investigators. Telegrams were sent to San Francisco requesting information from California authorities pertaining to important aspects in the case to date. All involved in this case, especially the detectives in the case awaited the arrival of John P. Dunning as it is presumed that he would be able to establish a link between the written materials and perhaps the perpetrator. By this point there were few people in Dover who believed that the person responsible for the deaths of Ida Henrietta Deane and Mary Elizabeth Dunning lived anywhere in the vicinity. Mr. Pennington had been of the steadfast belief as he had followed the investigation that the answer to this horrible crime lay elsewhere and that there was "nothing to investigate in the East." Circumstances dictated that no stone go unturned and the initial steps had included speaking with the postmaster at the Dover Post Office concerning his recollections of the "mysterious package."

Thomas Gooden, postmaster, recalled the arrival of the package, stating it came on the 5:58 P.M. train. He noticed no peculiarity about it. Mrs. Dunning had often received packages. He did note that "the boy" had picked up the box sometime before 8:00 P.M. on the 9th of August. There was a question due to the box's condition, which was reasonably pristine as to how far it had traveled. Police detectives in Delaware in conjunction with the authority of the attorney general were in close contact with Chief Lees of the San Francisco Police Department almost from the onset of the investigation. The Mrs. C referred to in the note found with the candy was of great interest to them. Friends of the Dunnings, associates, and co-workers in the Bay area were being sought to determine who this mystery woman might be.

August 20, 1898, saw the arrival of Mr. John P. Dunning, husband of the deceased Mary Elizabeth in Dover. Having been told of the full circumstances surrounding her death, he was secreted within the walls of-his father-in-law John B. Pennington's residence. Little was said concerning any conversations they may have had. As the public clamored for answers, Mr. Dunning steadfastly refused to make any statements. It was known that he had met with State Detective McVey, but the essence of their meetings was unknown.

It could be surmised with little difficulty that he had been shown the suspect writings in the possession of Mr. Pennington. Detective McVey, it was assumed because of his tenacity, had been able to attain vital clues which would tighten the noose around the fiend's neck. After long hours of consultation, John Dunning admitted to a liaison with a San Francisco woman. The name was transmitted by telegraph to Chief Lees who was taking the necessary steps to begin his connective half of the investigation.

Just how John P. Dunning, a respected newspaperman, became tangled in this web of vulgarity was still being questioned. Born in Middletown, Delaware, Dunning had studied law and, in fact, was admitted to the Bar of the State of Delaware. Life as a lawyer was not what he had envisioned. He therefore left the practice to become a reporter for the *Wilmington Morning News.*

Later employed by the Associated Press, John Dunning gained national prominence in 1889 for his reporting of the incident which occurred in the Samoan Islands, where it was feared there might be a clash of arms between American, British, and German warships. During the typhoon of March 16, 1889, when tensions had reached a fever pitch, Dunning cabled the exclusive story to the Associated Press, which was conceded by all to be a masterpiece of journalistic writing.

As a result, when he returned home he was made manager of the Associated Press in San Francisco. He returned home briefly and at some point courted Mary Elizabeth Pennington. They married in February of 1891 and went west to live. A child, little Mary, was born later the same year. Life at least on the surface appeared to have been rosy.

John Dunning, the man, had a dark side, which was hidden from those who were nearest and dearest. He can be best described as an enigma. For hidden from public views was a man, who as time would bare out, was a drunkard, gambler, and panhandling womanizer lost in the sea of excess. It was this need for the worldly life that had led to the double tragedy in Dover. As the evidence would bring out this penchant for excitement led him on a course which would end ultimately in disaster.

With the facts in hand, Bernard McVey, after a consultation with Attorney General-White, prepared for the arduous trek across the country to San Francisco. The facts known at present did point to that city as the repository for all the unanswered questions bearing on the case.

As McVey left the house of John Pennington, he carried a package presumably containing the evidence thus far collected in the case. One question still remained pertaining to the investigation in

Dover. Should the bodies of Mary Elizabeth and Ida Henrietta be exhumed and an autopsy performed? After much contemplation, which included lengthy discussions with Dr. Lemuel Bishop and Coroner Walls, Attorney-General Robert White decided against the exhumation of the bodies. The debate had been heated between these learned men. At its conclusion, the decision, of which all were in concurrence, was that an autopsy at this date would be fruitless. The bodies of the two deceased women had been embalmed. The embalming agent of the late nineteenth century was *arsenic.* Therefore by this time, every fiber of the bodies would be permeated with the lethal solution.

With the facts and evidence thus far collected in hand, Bernard McVey boarded a train in Dover for the circuitous trip west. The date was Tuesday, August 23, and it would be a long strenuous journey which would consume the better part of five days. The investigation, however, would not cease for San Francisco authorities were already moving forward checking initial clues given them by Delaware and narrowing the list of possible suspects. Initially, four women's names had risen in the investigation, and it was necessary to eliminate their involvement.

Chapter Four

Mystery Veils Darkly Mrs. Dunning's Slayer

From the onset of the investigation into the murders of Mary Elizabeth and Ida, all efforts were directed locating the enigmatic Mrs. C who may have sent the mysterious package. Within three days of the deaths, August 16, 1898, the *San Francisco Examiner* had tracked down Laura Corbalay, an intimate friend, of Mrs. Dunning while the latter had resided in San Francisco. Mrs. Corbalay was much distressed by the fact that she might been suspected of sending the deadly sweets east.

She thanked the *Examiner* for finding her and said she welcomed the opportunity to clear her name. Laura Corbalay gave a detailed statement to the reporter concerning the events surrounding her friend's death. There is a point within her statement, which is somewhat perplexing. Near the end of her statement she stopped, bowed her head in her hands and then suddenly looked up. After some degree of contemplation she stated:

> . . . Suppose a friend of Mrs. Dunning sent the candy with the best intentions, not knowing it contained a poisonous substance, do you think the public would accept the explanation and judge leniently if the sender should make an explanation? (*San Francisco Examiner* August 16, 1898).

Mrs. Corbalay also addressed two additional points of significance of her interview. The first is this: "What puzzles me is that the sender inserted the inscription Mrs. C; was it the intention to cast suspicion on me or was the initial just selected at random? The other point, which is far more telling, and which was to come out at a future point, was something which would appear at the time to be unrelated. It was, however, something that would have a far-reaching effect in revealing the murderer.

Mrs. Corbalay espoused a specific eccentricity of Mary Elizabeth Dunning regarding her likes and dislikes. It was that the murderer must have known that she had one weakness in her life. Mrs. Dunning was, according to Laura Corbalay, *extremely fond of candy* and, whenever Mary would travel downtown, she would buy a box to indulge this passion. Mrs. Corbalay was pronounced in her belief that sending chocolate to Mary Elizabeth Dunning would be like sending coal to New Castle.

This statement, as well as, a testament from Joshua Deane, husband of Ida Henrietta, was enough to remove Laura Corbalay from further suspicion. In his mind, Joshua was convinced that Laura Corbalay was free from guilt in this fiendish plot. Two letters had been received expressing first horror that her name had been intimated as the perpetrator and second her heartfelt sympathy and condolences for his loss. Both engendered a feeling within Joshua Deane that she was innocent and instilled a confidence within him. The police in San Francisco searched no further for the anonymous Mrs. C. They instead refocused their investigation on Cordelia Ada Botkin, a known associate of John P. Dunning.

As early as August 16, 1898, the name of Mrs. Cordelia A. Botkin, also known as Ada C. Botkin, had arisen in the case. Though not confirmed, it would appear that information obtained in Delaware through John P. Dunning had led to the inquiries which followed. One part is perplexing. Dunning had not arrived in Dover until the 20th of August, so it is possible that information regarding Mrs. Botkin was attained independently and perhaps coincidentally. The hows and whys of their early association are sketchy, but she was interviewed by the news media on August 16, 1898, which predates any involvement by John Dunning. She gave at this time the first of a number of statements prior to the trial which appear to be contradictory.

On August 16, 1898, Mrs. D. A. Botkin, as she was referred to at this time stated:

> I have been completely unnerved by the sad death of Mrs. Dunning through the sympathy, *pure and simple*, I had for her husband and which now goes out to the entire family. Surely she had no enemies in this part of the country. I first met Mr. Dunning in Golden Gate Park about a year and a half ago. I was sitting in the park with a lady friend when Mr. Dunning, then unknown to me, came along on his wheel. Just about the time he reached us his wheel broke and he stopped to repair it. He came over to where we were and sitting down beside us opened a conversation. I did not meet Mr. Dunning again until four or five months later, when I met him at the race course at Ingleside, where I had been accompanied by a lady and gentlemen. He came up to us and asked how we were succeeding and chatted on about unimportant topics for a time.
>
> Soon after that I invited Mr. Dunning to a quiet card party at my rooms at 927 Geary Street, where I made my home with my twenty-four-year-old son, Beverly Botkin. That evening the matter of Mr. Dunning's changing his apartments was discussed. He was then living on Post Street. His rooms were some three flights up, and he said he preferred apartments in a more private house. Acting on our advice, he decided to rent the small hall bedroom in the house where we roomed. From then on we spent many of our evenings together–usually, parties of four or six playing cards. I soon learned of the financial troubles of Mr. Dunning, he having lost very heavily on the races. His fear that his financial misfortune would revert against his family prayed heavily on his mind. He idolized his wife and child to such an extent that he would weep by the hour over the unhappiness he seemed to feel surrounding their lot (*San Francisco Examiner,* August 16, 1898).

It was also during this initial period that Cordelia Botkin intimated that there might have been two other women who could have motives for bringing her name into the investigation. The names of these women were Mrs. Clara Arbogast and Mrs. Louise Seeley. Her reasoning for the first was that she was intimate with Cordelia's husband and sought to remove her. The latter's motive revolved around the relationship that Seeley had with Cordelia's son, Beverly. Cordelia has shown disdain concerning this liaison, and thus she felt Mrs. Seeley might have been vengeful. Both names would surface again as time progressed. Questions which arise as one delves into the case abound. On the surface, appearances would seem to point to the fact that Cordelia Botkin was an unassuming, naïve dupe, who through no fault of her own had become involved in a complex murder plot. It is fundamentally important to digress at this juncture, to ascertain exactly who she was, what direction her life had taken, and what, if any, was her motivation?

Due to the number of years, which have passed, the life of Cordelia Botkin is limited. She spoke little of herself and her formative years. What is known is that she was born Adelaide Cordelia Brown sometime in 1854 in Brownsville, Nebraska. The Browns were a family of social standing in the heartland of America. She and her sisters stressed very strongly that they were a family of English descent and were known to affect a stature which placed them above commoners in society. She married a gentleman of some social standing in the community named Welcome A. Botkin in 1872. Beginning life as a bank teller, he had risen in life through investments. Ventures into the grain market as a broker had suited him well. The affluent couple had lived in Kansas City for years and then in the 1880s they had removed to Stockton, California, with their son, Beverly. Coincidentally, at the same time, most of the Brown family came west also and began settling in various towns of Northern California. (San Francisco Murders)

The sedentary life of homemaker did not suit Cordelia. She was not one to sit tamely at home and allow herself to collect moss. At times she ventured to the homes of various relatives and on other occasions she lived, by herself or with Beverly, at various locations in the city of San Francisco. She received an allowance from Welcome A. Botkin, which enabled her to have an extremely pleasant life. Divorce was never an issue, and it appears that Mr. Botkin was not unduly unhappy by Cordelia's departures.

As facts would bear out in the near future, this freedom of movement brought about the chance meeting, which brought John Dunning into her life. It was as Cordelia pointed out, and John P. Dunning would later confirm, an innocent meeting of two people in September of 1895. On that day, the chance encounter in Golden Gate Park, set in motion the events three years hence which had such murderous results.

Recall if you will Cordelia's initial statement of August 16:

> I first met Mr. Dunning in Golden Gate Park (sometime previous). I was sitting in the park with a lady friend when Mr. Dunning, then unknown to me, came along on his wheel (bicycle). Just about the time he reached us his wheel broke and he stopped to repair it. He came over to me and engaged in conversation (*San Francisco Examiner,* August 16, 1898).

Early on as the investigation was just beginning, the newspapers were already aware of Cordelia. During a two day period, August 15 and 16, while staying at her sister's home in Healdsburg she gave interviews to Lizzie Livernash, of the *San Francisco Examiner.* Cordelia Botkin made numerous curious admissions during this time. These admissions were made in response to the reporter intimating that Cordelia Botkin was already suspected of sending the poisoned chocolates.

She related that it must have been an accident, and unknown to the sender, the chocolates contained poison and the transmission of them was accidental. Mrs. Botkin readily admitted to her relationship with John P. Dunning but stated that it was platonic. She wavered between self-pity, shock, hysteria, and righteous indignation. Reading the accounts as written, one senses or denotes the unraveling of a Shakespearean-like tragedy. Lady Macbeth would have been a role well suited for Cordelia Botkin. At one point, Cordelia thought that she should speak no more until she acquired legal counsel. Acquiescing to the interview, Cordelia made perhaps her most damming declaration. "Oh why," she said, "didn't I let the man die? Better have let the man die and spare the mother to her child."

It was during these interviews that Cordelia's son Beverly came into the room. With no external solicitation he began to espouse his views concerning the good times which abounded in his mother's company. Unchecked, Beverly related some of the seamy aspects of the life and times at 927 Geary Street. Dramatically, almost oft handedly, Beverly stated that "Jack Dunning loves my mother and (my mother) has affection for him." Cordelia became hysterical and in a distressful voice stated, "Oh what shall I do? My son has the power to damn me?"

This interview alone, for it is doubtful that the police did not read the papers, pointed the finger of fate at Cordelia Botkin. She, however, was not through and, for whatever reason managed to keep herself in the limelight. Among other things in her life, Cordelia Botkin spoke of receiving "anonymous letters" which threatened her own person "to the extreme." According to her, in light of the present trauma which she faced, she wished she had not destroyed them (*San Francisco Examiner,* August 23, 1898).

On the 23rd of August, while Bernard McVey, state detective from Delaware, was still en route, the San Francisco Police moved, independent of Delaware, and issued an arrest warrant for Mrs. Ada Botkin. Speaking for the first time their warrant was based on the following:

> In the Police Court of the City and County of San Francisco, State of California. The People of the State of California vs. Mrs. Ada Botkin–Felony, to wit: Murder. A fugitive from Justice. State of California, City and County of San Francisco.
>
> Personally appeared before me this 23d day of August A.D. 1898, E. L. Gibson, who, on oath, upon information and belief, makes complaint and deposes and says:
>
> That on the 11th day of August, A.D. 1898, in the County of Kent, State of Delaware, the crime of felony, to wit: Murder, was committed by Mrs. Ada Botkin, who did then and there, willfully, unlawfully, feloniously and of her malice aforethought, kill and murder a human being, to wit:
>
> Mrs. J. P. Dunning, and this affiant here and now sets forth the facts upon which his said information and belief are founded:
>
> That on the 23d day of August, A.D. 1898, a telegram was received by I. W. Lees, Chief of Police of the City and County of San Francisco, which was then and there in the words and figures, as follows, to wit:
>
> "Dated Dover, Delaware, August 22, 1898.-To Chief of Police, S. F.: Arrest Ada Botkin, 927 Geary street; also English lady, same place. Intercept letter from Dover to Ada Botkin. Wire me upon arrest. Hold for requisition. R. C. WHITE, Attorney-General."

That on the 22d day of August, 1898, Chief of Police of said City and County of San Francisco sent the following telegram, to wit:

"San Francisco, Aug. 22, 1898–R. C. White, Attorney-General, Dover, Delaware: Mrs. D. A. Botkin is temporarily in San Joaquin county. Telegraph following facts necessary to enable me to make complaint and obtain warrant for her arrest, and hold as a fugitive under our statute: Crime charged; date of complaint; name of Judge issuing; title of court; name of official to whom warrant is directed; date of commission of crime; where crime alleged. I. W. LEES, Chief of Police."

In response to which, said Chief of Police of said City and County of San Francisco received the following telegram:

"Dated Georgetown, Delaware, August 23d, 1898, 12 m-To Chief of Police, S. F.: Crime charged, murder; complaint made August 23d, before Peter L. Cooper, Justice of Peace; warrant directed to Constable: crime committed August 11th, at Kent county, Delaware; messenger with evidence on way. R. C. WHITE, Attorney-General."

And that on said information this affiant makes this complaint, and alleges the facts to be, that said crime of felony, to wit: murder, has been committed by said Mrs. Ada Botkin as hereinabove alleged, that said Mrs. Ada Botkin has been charged in said foreign State, to wit: said State of Delaware, with the commission of said crime, and that a criminal prosecution according to the laws of 'the said State of Delaware has been commenced and is now pending in said State of Delaware against said Mrs. Ada Botkin, and the said Mrs. Ada Botkin ever since the commission of said crime has been, and is now, a fugitive from the justice of said State of Delaware, and has been and is now, found within the State of California.

All of which is contrary to the form, force and effect of the Statute in such case made and provided, and against the peace and dignity of the People of the State of California, and this complainant upon oath accuses the said Mrs. Ada Botkin of having committed the said crime, and this complainant further prays that the said accused may be brought before a magistrate and dealt with according to law.

(Signed.) E. L. GIBSON

Subscribed and sworn to before me this 23d day of August, 1898.

H. L. JOACHIMSEN,
Judge of the Police Court of the City and County of San Francisco.

The people of the State of California vs. Mrs. Ada Botkin, a fugitive from justice. Complainant, E. L. Gibson. Filed in the Police Court of the City and County of San Francisco this 23d day of August (1898 *San Francisco Examiner,* August 24, 1898).

Detective Edward Gibson of the San Francisco Police Department and Chief Gall of the Stockton Police Department were given the task of executing the warrants. As they read the warrants charging her with the two Delaware murders Cordelia became unnerved. She sprang to her feet and it appeared, at any moment that she would become uncontrollable. Quickly, Cordelia regained her composure and stated with a huff at the conclusion of reading, "Well the excitement has worn off, I am now prepared for anything."

Having been read the charges which the State of Delaware had brought against her, the helpless Mrs. Botkin was allowed time to prepare herself and then was taken to the Stockton jail to await transportation the following day to San Francisco. She asked almost innocently what events she was facing, as if the totality of the circumstances were unknown to her. It was indeed a tense and somber scene, which under a different setting would merit applause. When told that she would be placed on trial for her life, her response was melodramatic. "For my life, for my life, my God!!" Regaining her senses Cordelia, in matter of fact tones, orchestrated the packing of her trunk prior to leaving. She in all respects was a very remarkable and calculating woman.

In retrospect, one can say that this was certainly true. With all that she faced, Cordelia Botkin was able to muster theories of her own regarding the mysterious package and its poisoned contents. To the astonishment of all, she hypothesized the following:

> Now, how do they know the candy was poisoned with intent? Did you ever know that when candy is sent a long distance, a poison is germinated?. . . .I wonder why the doctors have not thought of that theory.

Switching tactics, Cordelia then proposed a solution concerning the note. She queried that:

> Now might it not be possible that it was written by some of my enemies and that it might have been forged? It might have been written in a nervous manner, which would make it hard to discover the similarity between a forgery and the genuine (*San Francisco Examiner,* August 24, 1898).

Beyond Cordelia, there were two questions that the Delaware and San Francisco police had prior to the arrest of Mrs. Botkin, but they were extremely important. One was what woman was there in San Francisco who might, actuated by regard for Dunning, wish his wife out of the way? Second, with whom had Dunning been intimate while residing in San Francisco?

It was very clear to anyone even remotely associated with this case that the guilt or innocence of Cordelia Botkin could not be solely based on these issues. Probable cause was established and as the case progressed if malice was to be ruled out, then in this case it left but one reason, jealousy. The case before the investigators was thus at this stage. The initial pieces of the jigsaw puzzle had fallen into place but a chain of evidence, direct or circumstantial, was necessary before the case would reach fruition. Therefore as Cordelia Botkin languished in the county jail, the police moved onward to forge the chain which would prove the theories upon which their initial case was based.

Chapter Five

Trailing the Track of the Dover Assassin

Despite the distance involved between the crime scene in Dover, Delaware, and the person allegedly responsible for the act in San Francisco, the police on both ends did an admirable job. They were working in an age which had only the rudiments of communications. The device known as the telephone, which we take for granted, was in its infancy. In this age the mainstay of life was the telegraph. This aside, within two weeks they had realized a crime of immense proportion had occurred and had moved in concert to find the solution to the heinous, malicious act. The evidence collected in the East was being brought to the City by the Bay and would arrive within days. The question remains to this day, however; did they rush to judgment?

They had little or no concrete evidence with the exception of John P. Dunning's suspicions which were related in confidence to the Delaware authorities. Dunning had apparently made admissions, but these were not public knowledge. In realistic terms, the case to this point was an illusion. Police based their case on the premise that the package came from San Francisco. There were contradictory statements made by Cordelia, but these were only alleged, not proven. There was to the untrained observer very little as a basis for an arrest for murder.

Now in his custody, Chief I. W. Lees of the San Francisco Police Department interviewed Cordelia Botkin for the first time. She spoke quietly and calmly and chose every word carefully. Her story changed significantly through the course of the interview and began with a general discourse of her life. Completing this, Cordelia launched into an unequivocal denial of the charges and a sweeping refutation of all the interviews, which had been previously published.

Cordelia Botkin went so far as to say that she had not been in a candy store *anywhere* for the past eighteen months. She revealed that her last candy purchase was for a nephew and even described the purchase as a bag of lemon drops. In great detail she expounded upon her movements from July 27 until her arrest on August 24, 1898. Having completed the interview, it would be sometime before she spoke again to the police or for any publication. At the conclusion of her interview, Cordelia addressed Chief Lees directly. "Now I am here, and I have told you all I know about the case." (*The Call*, August 25, 1898). She threw down the gauntlet to both the police and reporters as if to say, "If you think I did this awful deed, prove it (in court)."

Bernard McVey was still a good two days from San Francisco when good fortune appeared to smile upon the police who were making very little headway in verifying their premise concerning the investigation. Frank Gattrell of the Wave Candy Store in Stockton, California, stated that three weeks prior, a woman whose description was identical to Cordelia Botkin purchased a box of candy at his establishment. She had not been seen since in the city. Coincidentally, Cordelia was staying in Stockton on July 27, 28, and 29, which was approximately three weeks previous to August 24.

This, if proven, could have been a damning piece of evidence for the prosecution of Cordelia. Unfortunately for the police, the clue did not bare fruit as neither Mr. Gattrell nor a co-worker were able to identify either Cordelia Botkin or the box of candy when given the opportunity. Chief Lees was left at this point with one less piece of evidence, which was a red herring and brought him personal embarrassment and the wrath of the press and Cordelia's attorneys.

It was left to the Delaware officials to make public their reasoning as to why they felt Cordelia Botkin was guilty of this amoral and depraved act. Where John Dunning had been reluctant to speak on the subject, Attorney-General Robert C. White was reticent. He stated, in part:

> Dunning made a clean breast of it to me. He held nothing back. He was as sincere as he could be in his desire to bring the fiendish murderess to justice. The moment he was shown the anonymous letters that were sent from San Francisco to Mrs. Dunning . . . he recognized the handwriting and said it was Mrs. Botkin. We had already been on her trail and that statement from Dunning made us doubly confident...In a like manner Dunning identified the writing on the wrapper and the note enclosed (*The Call,* August 25, 1898).

Delaware did have the vital clues and by bringing them to light saved Chief Lees from further ridicule. The case, indeed, was on the right track.

After his laborious trek across the United States, Bernard McVey arrived in San Francisco. The date was August 28, and it was felt that now the investigations which had been sidetracked would be reinvigorated, move in a fruitful direction, and would result in a positive outcome. Reporters besieged McVey incessantly as he neared his final destination. To his credit Detective McVey steadfastly refused to answer questions posed to him and warned San Francisco officials to do likewise. His reasoning was, as always, sound and symbolized true professionalism.

Speaking too freely at this juncture could jeopardize and interfere with his reason for coming to the Pacific Coast. His only statement was that "I have what I believe is very important evidence in the case...My only hope is to strengthen the case . . . by adding, combining, and comparing what I have to what San Francisco officials have gathered." (*The Call,* August 28, 1898). After a day of rest north of San Francisco, McVey embarked for police headquarters. The officer's only statement prior to entering into conference with Chief Lees was "the people of the State of Delaware will have no peace until the poisoner is brought to justice." (*The Call,* August 28, 1898).

Closely guarded by McVey was the satchel which contained numerous items of evidence. As described, the point of main interest for now was the wrapper, the box and the miscellaneous contents. It consisted in part of a dainty handkerchief of lace with a price tag of twenty-five cents attached. The package itself, which was an ordinary bonbon box, pink in color, with the gilded letters in script BON BONS. At each end was a pink silk ribbon. The box measured seven and one-half inches by three and three quarters inches, and was one and seven-eighths inches deep.

Contained within the box were the deadly chocolates which were of varying types. The wrapper to the box was nondescript. The words, "Mrs. John P. Dunning, Dover," appeared in duplicate. Delewere, it should be noted again, was misspelled. There were five cancelled stamps in the upper right hand corner and the partial postmark San Francisco could be plainly seen. In addition to the deadly candies was a note, on paper, or rather a scrap torn from a much larger piece. The death note contained the simple phrase "With love to yourself and baby, Mrs. C."

While the examination was taking place at police headquarters, Cordelia Botkin decided to take it upon herself to break her self-imposed silence. She issued this statement to the editor of *The Call:*

> I believe the time has arrived when it is proper for me to speak, and I take this method of requesting you to publish in your columns the following statement: Up to the present time I have maintained silence by the advice of my husband, who told me when this awful suspicion was first brought upon me that in my hysterical and terrified condition talking could do me no good, and that anything I might say would undoubtedly be distorted and misrepresented and perhaps used to my disadvantage by the sensational reporters.
>
> Since I have obtained legal counsel, I have been told that this advice was good. Therefore it has been through no desire to keep from the public information of my defense in this matter that I have remained silent under the most trying circumstances stances, but because in the humiliation and terror of being arrested on suspicion of having committed an awful crime, I felt that it was not safe for me to speak.
>
> Now, however, my friends, to whom I have given a history of my life for years past, advise me that I ought to at least publicly assert my innocence. To those who know me and know that I am incapable of committing any such crime as has been laid at my door, I need say nothing. They will not believe a word against me. To strangers, who may think the newspaper reporters have made out a case against me, I only ask what should be granted to every accused person–a suspension of opinion until I can be heard in court.

I am a woman and almost defenseless. I am prostrated with grief and humiliation. I am filled with horror at the position in which I am placed. Is it unreasonable under these circumstances to ask those who do not know me to await the hearing? If given an opportunity I shall prove my innocence, for I am innocent before God.

I have told Chief of Police Lees everything. I have accounted for every moment of my life for months past. I have told one of my attorneys, Senator McGowan, the whole story of my life. He believes me innocent and says I need have no fear that harm will come to me. I thank heaven that at least one strong and resolute man is prepared to defend me with all his talent, and the authorities of this city, who should ever sustain the weak and defenseless, seem leagued against me.

I do not know the wife of John P. Dunning and have no feeling against her. I am not and never was in love with Mr. Dunning. I befriended him when he was in trouble, and that is all. My son was very fond of him and both of us believe that he is a true gentlemen and that none of the things he is reported to have told the Delaware officers against me are true.

I am incapable of committing any such crime as this. My relations with Mr. Dunning were only those of a friend. I never wrote him love letters, nor has he written me such letters. Chief Lees has all my letters, including those written by my husband for a year past, and they contain nothing which shows me in any other than a proper light.

What more can I say? I deny everything. Can it be possible that I am to be convicted by the newspapers of a crime of which I am innocent, simply because I was unfortunate as to enjoy the acquaintance of John P. Dunning and to help him in his financial troubles?

What possible motive could I have for poisoning his wife? He has told me that she was a lovely woman and that he thought more her than he could tell. I respected him for that. I was not responsible for his troubles. I only did for him what other friends did for him while he resided in San Francisco. I aided him in my weak and humble way to retrieve his fortunes.

I have said all this, not because I expect to be believed, for I know that every hand is raised against a helpless woman in my position, but because I can no longer restrain my emotions. In due time I know I shall come out of this ordeal unscathed. I am confident that a just God will not permit an innocent woman to suffer and I have faith in him.

I have read about innocent person having been convicted upon circumstantial evidence which afterward turned out to be misleading and untrue, and the thought that I may become a victim of such a thing fills me with horror and dismay. But I shall try to bear up and meet manfully whatever fate shall have in store for me, conscious in my heart that I am innocent and that the truth will in the end vindicate me.

Will you please publish this? You have given columns to my prosecutors. Please give me a word in reply. Signed–Cordelia Botkin.

The Call, August 30, 1898

Cordelia had as she would be prone to do throughout the entire case expressed her opinions and had expounded upon her virtuous nature.

Conversely, the police having concluded their initial conference and leaving the evidence in the custody of Chief Lees, quietly set about retracing the steps taken to date in the investigation. As all good detectives will, Detectives McVey and Gibson showed a tenacious effort working in concert to ferret all the vital clues.

These two men, one from the East the other the West, were of a common breed. Bernard McVey was described as fair type for his calling. Quiet of manner, plain in appearance, he matched in personality dozens of his counterparts that could be met at the police headquarters of any large city. He was a stalwart figure and had strong features. Twenty-one of his forty-years had been spent in police work. Born in Delaware, he was known in eastern police circles as a shrewd and courageous officer.

He and Edward Gibson meshed perfectly as hunters of men and the occasional woman. Though they had never met, a bond was fused from their first encounter. Instinctively they recognized each other as members of the same profession upon McVey's arrival in San Francisco. Gibson explained "I can smell a 'copper' a block away." McVey was more eloquent in his determination. He could "pick a detective from others and men similarly attired. A man does not remain long at the trade without acquiring certain characteristics of face and manner."

Thus the two working in concert began their task of tracking the evidence, while other detectives branched out to find key witnesses and, between the two groups, bring the case against Cordelia Botkin to closure. As September began, the detectives involved in the investigation had begun revisiting all the drug stores in the city in an attempt to locate the point of purchase of the arsenic. After two dismal days of contacting all available drug stores, they had reached the point of giving up the ghost.

Late in the afternoon of September 3, word was received that this crucial missing link may have been found. The detectives McVey, Gibson, and their cohorts responded to the Owl Drug Store, 1128 Market Street. The story lay before them in a simple entry in the record book:

"6-1-98 2 P.M. Mrs. Bothin Cal &
Hyde Sts. arsenic 311; Bleaching. Grey.

(A translation of entry means that on June 1, 1898, at 2 P.M., Mrs. Bothin living at California and Hyde Streets bought two ounces of arsenic for purpose of bleaching. Grey is the clerk who sold it to her).

Frank Grey remembered the sale but stated it had simply slipped his memory. When originally asked by the police their concern had been referenced for sales July 1 or after. Mr. Grey stated regarding this particular sale, he had questioned the customer as to the use, and she had told him it was to bleach a straw hat. Therefore it was clearly embedded in his mind. (*The Examiner,* September 4, 1898). The use struck him as odd, for he had never heard of arsenic being used for that purpose. He tried to sell the lady something less dangerous, but she had been adamant in her request. As arsenic is a lethal substance, notation of all sales was mandated by law, though sale of the substance was allowable without a prescription.

Frank Grey went further: The customer who purchased the arsenic on the date in question was no stranger. His former employment had been with the Baldwin Pharmacy, and he had met her on numerous prior occasions. Though Grey wrote "Bothin" rather than "Botkin," this was explained by Grey from the way she spelled the name. Grey was positive if he saw the lady in question face to face he could identify her.

The police were satisfied they now had a concrete clue. Not only could the druggist identify the suspect, they had the name. So close in spelling, it was inconceivable to think there could be an error. To reinforce the matter was the last piece of information which made it conclusive. At the time of the purchase Cordelia Botkin's address was Victoria Hotel–at the corner of California and Hyde Streets.

The next task for the detective was to trace the fancy handkerchief which had been placed in the box. As mentioned, the small paper price tag was still attached to it when the box was opened. Simultaneous to this search was the tracing of the candy back to its source. Ostensibly possessing the knowledge that the only candy manufacturer to use such a box was the George Haas Candy Company, it is difficult to understand what took them so long.

More confusing still is the fact that the police spent two days interviewing and displaying the candy and box to employees at various confections shops. Perhaps the San Francisco Police did not believe that a small town detective had ferreted such a vital clue, or perhaps they were testing McVey and the Delaware authorities for investigative correctness. Finally, when they spoke to the clerks at the Haas establishment, one readily recognized the box. Mr. George Haas, owner of the shop at 810 Market Street, was then contacted and stated, "I recognized not only the box but also the candy as soon as it was shown to me. We are the only people who use the box, which is made by Jones and Co. of Philadelphia." (*The Call*, September 2, 1898). Good fortune had led them to the candy store. A much more difficult task lay ahead, however: locating a clerk who remembered selling the box. Eventually, through persistence though not for some time, they would locate a witness who would tie the box to Cordelia Botkin.

Having accomplished this, the investigation was directed to the handkerchief. Investigators moved on a steady course, beginning with inquiries at the various dry good stores throughout the city. Chief Lees himself thoroughly immersed in the inquiry took the handkerchief to "The City Of Paris." It was immediately identified as merchandise which had been on sale at the store for nearly a year. The price mark was identified by store manager as coming from The City of Paris. Another vital clue was thus identified. The City of Paris was a fashionable establishment and was known to have been frequented by Mrs. Botkin. She was well-known as a shopper and also for cashing postal orders at the cashier's desk. It was also established that in the company of a future witness, Cordelia had shown interest in a fancy handkerchief prior to the murders. Cordelia had noted the price on the handkerchief and indicated her desire to have one. The handkerchiefs the witness would note were much like the one in evidence.

At this point from her rooms at the county jail, Cordelia made another admission to an unnamed friend (this person was never identified which was indeed fortunate) who was visiting. She stated that Frank Grey would not have to identify her. She admitted to purchasing two ounces of arsenic on June 1 for the purpose, which she had stated, of bleaching. She stated that she did use it to bleach a hat. She further stated that in fact she knew Frank Grey from his days at the Baldwin Pharmacy. Cordelia said that she often sought Grey out when she was in need of prescriptive medications because of their past association.

Cordelia went so far as to state that she had two witnesses (friends) who were with her at the time of the arsenic purchase. The witnesses are reputable according to Cordelia and would substantiate what she had claimed in court. She wanted neither name released at this time for fear the press would harass them, but she had given the names to her attorneys. (Note: Neither of these witnesses ever appeared at any of the criminal proceedings for the defense).

As the case proceeded, the physical evidence was beginning to accumulate and the prosecution began to stiffen in its resolve. The physical evidence to date against Cordelia Botkin was encouraging and consisted of the following listed items:

1. The Candy Box	Jones and Co. of Philadelphia to George Haas Candy Company
2. The Candy	Identified by George Haas
3. The Handkerchief	City of Paris
4. Arsenic	Frank Grey at Owl Drugs
5. Box Wrapper Writing	Both written by Cordelia Botkin according to J. P. Dunning
6. Anonymous Letter Writing	
7. Known Handwriting	Cordelia Botkin for comparison by experts

As Cordelia freely now admitted to the arsenic purchase, close attention was turned to the types of arsenic which were in the candy. It was important for the prosecution to describe the type of arsenic in the candy for conviction, and in this endeavor great lengths were taken. Analysis and re-analysis was needed to make a proper determination as to whether the arsenic was crystalline or powdered.

On September 13, they benefited from another scrap of evidence and which would assist them in completing the evidentiary puzzle Mr. W. W. Barnes was showing the room once occupied by Cordelia Botkin to a prospective roomer. Independent of each other, Mr. Barnes and the inquiring boarder, William Rosello, noticed a portion of a George Haas Candy Company seal sticking out from under the carpet by the sofa. The seal, which was bronze in color and had a quatrefoil design, was very identifiable. Strings of mingled silver and rose were still fastened in place. It was evident upon examinations that the seal had been cut from a George Haas and Son Package. (*Delaware Gazette and State Journal,* September *15,* 1898). How it had come to remain in the room was somewhat perplexing. There had been, at least, two subsequent occupants since Cordelia's departure from the Victoria Hotel and the room had been cleaned on each occasion. Its presence was not readily explainable, but it did offer another point of fact in the growing set of coincidences.

The last piece of evidence in the puzzle needed for a successful prosecution was a professional and expert analysis of the handwriting. Possessing both unknown samples, the candy wrapper and note, and known samples of Cordelia Botkin's writing, the stage was set for the examination. It was a fittingly dramatic conclusion to a case which was built upon the miniscule, one detail at a time. The question remained however, would the results of this very instrumental examination be *positive or negative.*

Chirography (handwriting analysis) was held in much higher repute in the nineteenth century than it is in the modern age. Today it is considered more of an art form than incontrovertible evidence. The police were ultimately to rely on three separate experts in the area to gain the testimony which would seal Cordelia's fate. As early as September 15, word had been received that "Experts positively identify paper on inside of box as Mrs. Botkin's." (*Delaware Gazette and State Journal,* September 15, 1898). Though somewhat prematurely reported, the results in the end would bear out the published report.

With the physical evidence needed for prosecution acquired, the police began the search for those witnesses that would collaborate and sustain the chain of circumstances they had forged. It has often been said that physical evidence can be very strong standing by itself, the main benefit is that evidence can not lie, it cannot be totally absent, and it cannot perjure itself. There is one drawback, however: It cannot speak and must, therefore, rely upon humans with all their frailties to validate it.

With this in mind, the police now turned to these humans who would give life to their theories and suspicions. There were many witnesses to the events which had taken place and had been documented. Some would be of assistance, some would not, and some would be of more assistance than others. There were some who had no motive for becoming involved; others were, and still are, questionable. This, however, would be for a jury of Cordelia's peers to sort out at a date in the not so distant future.

Chapter Six

Mrs. Botkin Not a Fugitive from Delaware's Jurisdiction

The police function of collecting evidence and securing witnesses who would testify to their veracity was but one cog in the wheel of justice. Another side to the case was far more perplexing. This involved the legal aspects, and, as with the evidence, there was a good deal of wrangling. It was apparent from the outset that the Dunning/Deane murders would have a far-reaching effect on jurisprudence in the years to come.

Case law which exists today was almost nonexistent in the late nineteenth century. There had been no contingency set in stone for what had occurred. State governments and for that matter the federal government had to this point never thought of the legalities, which were to rise in the beginnings of this case. Who would have fathomed that a person 3,000 miles distant would be charged with causing the death of two innocent victims. Our founding fathers, in drafting the United States Constitution, never fathomed such a disgusting act. This is where the variance in law from the point of view of opposing sides rested.

The case from the State of Delaware's perspective was plain and simple. Determining that a crime had occurred and that the accused party was in custody, Delaware authorities began the initial phase, August *25,* 1898, of "procuring the body" for trial. A preliminary hearing was held in which all parties associated with the case in Delaware were formally deposed. Depositions from John Pennington and family, the doctors, postal employees, and the coroner were attached to the requisition order. This document was, at its completion, transmitted to the authorities in San Francisco.

Attorney-General White, speaking in Dover, stated emphatically that "We have the murderess of Mrs. Deane and Mrs. Dunning and she will be in Delaware within three weeks." (*Every Evening*, August 26, 1898). Unfortunately, problems were to be encountered with these papers from the beginning. The first set, sent by Governor Ebe Tunnell to Governor James H. Budd, were found to be faulty. To add to the problems faced by the Delaware authorities, Cordelia Botkin, through her husband, Welcome, had assembled a formidable defense team.

These attorneys, George Knight, Frank McGowan, and their associates, would place innumerable obstacles in the path of the prosecution. The crux of the matter was that Cordelia Botkin, having said on numerous occasions that she looked forward to the opportunity of freeing herself of the charges against her, now had a change of heart. Through her legal counsel, she began to wage a war through litigation to impede her removal from the State of California.

The contention of the defense was that Cordelia Botkin could not be taken from California and transported to Delaware as a fugitive from justice. Their reasoning, in this matter, was on sound footing. In order to be a fugitive, the accused had to have been in the State of Delaware when the crime occurred and therefore "constructively present." As George Knight succinctly put it before the court " . . . she has never been in the State of Delaware and therefore, cannot be a fugitive." (*Every Evening*, August 29, 1898).

"Constructively present" were words, which would be bantered over in the weeks to come as Governor James Budd was given the task of resolving the issue. To the layman of the period, this legalese must have been confusing. The law of extradition, however, was quite clear and had to be taken literally. A person committing a crime must be in the state where the crime occurred; if not, they could not be deemed to have fled, and therefore could not be extradited. The eyes of the legal community throughout the nation rested upon the State of California. A prominent lawyer in Chicago wrote that " . . . unless the laws of the State of California make the act of sending poisoned candy to Delaware with intent to commit murder a violation of the criminal code, the defendant couldn't be tried except in the State of Delaware." (*San Francisco Examiner*, August 27, 1898).

The attorney, James B. David, went on to state, however, that " . . . I find no law governing this in the statutes of California. . . . She never has been a fugitive from justice under Federal or California law and therefore cannot be extradited." (*San Francisco Examiner*, August 27, 1898).

It appears that our forefathers never envisioned such a chain of events as faced the California Legal system in 1898. In Article IV of the U. S. Constitution they had laid the groundwork upon which this case was based, and it was extremely clear. If this were not enough, there was case law, already founded, which did cover the case at hand. In *Hall v. People*, 115 N.C. 311, two men, Hall and Lockery were arrested in North Carolina for a murder in Tennessee. In a nutshell, Tennessee insisted that the two men had fired a fatal shot into the victim while he stood in North Carolina just across the border. The case had gone to the U. S. Supreme Court, which stated that they were not fugitives from Tennessee and therefore could not be extradited to North Carolina. Neither man was tried for the murder.

The prosecution, therefore, was fighting an uphill battle from the beginning. With legal precedent on the side of the defense, and Governor James Budd vacillating, the state's attorneys were in a perplexing dilemma. They searched for some means to persuade the governor that it would be in the best interest of the State of California to establish new legal precedent.

The prosecution and the police were appalled by the governor 's contention that the accused could be tried in the State of California, but not for murder. It was Governor Budd's suggestion that she be charged and tried for "mixing poison into food." To the police this was a ludicrous idea. If they were to acquiesce and sign warrants for food adulteration, they knew the results. Her attorneys would advise her to plead guilty and take her sentence, which by statute would be no more than two years, and that would be the end of the charges of murder against two innocent victims. Having this in mind the prosecution persevered against the odds with the faint hope of arriving at a just conclusion.

The governor of California did, in fact, issue a statement, which elated the defense. His contention was, and as pointed out, the California Constitution would not permit the extradition of Cordelia Botkin. This was indeed an extreme blow to the prosecution, but they vowed to push onward and make legal argument for her prosecution in the State of California. Chief Lees reacted by issuing this statement, when he heard of Cordelia's possible release. "Yes, Mrs. Botkin is in prison, but carry your mind back to the State of Delaware and see where two murdered women are lying in their graves forever." (*Every Evening*, September 27, 1898). He appealed to the governor and to the prosecutors with the thought that all the police wanted was a chance to show who did it.

For its part, the defense was filled with elation. They had won a smashing victory for their client, Cordelia Botkin. Upon receipt of the necessary paperwork from the police, and signed by Governor Budd, she would be released. As George Knight so succinctly voiced, "We have complied with the letter of the law." (*Every Evening*, September 27, 1898).

The state prosecutors had but one avenue left and this they used. An appeal of the governor's judgment was filed and the case was left to be resolved by a panel of justices. Their determination would set the course in the legal battle, which followed. As the Superior Court justices mulled over the question of freedom for Cordelia, extradition to Delaware, or trial by the State of California, an interesting event beyond the courtroom was about to come to light.

Rumors abounded in San Francisco, and the most prevalent must have reached Cordelia's ears. (*Every Evening*, October 12, 1898). She suddenly became very nervous and refused to leave her quarters in the county jail. Apparently she had become alarmed at a rumor. This rumor from an unknown source was that if not extradited to Delaware, a plan was afoot to kidnap her. Was this real or imagined?

Were these facts verifiable? It had been reported by the *Delaware Gazette and State Journal*, November 17, 1898, in an article entitled "Detective McVey Returns," that some point of truth may have been in the rumor. It was reported that. . . .

> When legal efforts to secure Mrs. Botkin seemed unavailing, a scheme was planned for the abduction of the woman after the granting of the extradition papers. The plan was to put her on board a tugboat and then convey her to a vessel for New York by way of Cape Horn (*Delaware Gazette and State Journal* November 17, 1898).

The key to the story lies in the statement "after extradition papers were signed." Though unconfirmed, it would appear that Delaware may have been willing to take extraordinary means to secure her person. Be that as it may, the legal battle for Cordelia between the two states was drawing to a conclusion. Events shortly would show this to be a moot point.

On October 24, 1898, the Superior Court consisting of five justices ruled that "Mrs. Cordelia Botkin will not be extradited to the State of Delaware." (*Every Evening*, October 25, 1898). In this final decree, the justices placed the onus on the State of California. Their conclusion was that if she (Cordelia) were to be tried for murder, it would have to be in this state.

Delaware was given no further legal ground in California. It was disheartening, but plans were immediately set in motion to appeal the decision to the U. S. Supreme Court. This would mean a lengthy legal battle in which Cordelia Botkin, who had seemingly won a victory, would be brought east for a hearing in Washington, D.C. Bernard McVey expressed the feeling that "If the California decision holds; it opens the way for murder by means of bombs or poison candy, if sent from one state to another, without punishment." (*Every Evening*, October 25, 1898).

With the extradition of Cordelia Botkin now set aside, the remaining action placed before the court was "Could she be tried by the State of California for murder?" A rather obscure entry in the California Penal Code (1872) under Section 27 indicated that she could. A date for arguments regarding this section of the statute was set. However, at this time George Knight then did a rather queer thing. Knight stated that he would "place no obstacles in the way of the prosecution bringing the matter to trial here . . . he was satisfied to let the prosecution proceed either before the grand jury or the Police Court." (*San Francisco Examiner*, October 25, 1898). The case was remanded to the grand jury on October 26, 1898, and it was charged with the authority to decide whether or not Cordelia Botkin would be tried for the murders of Elizabeth Dunning and Ida Deane.

Let us, for a moment, take leave of the legal debates which had taken center stage in the case. For it is interesting to revisit the accused and view how she was bearing under the circumstances. Cordelia, it was reported in *The Call*, "enjoys all the comforts of home in the city prison." The report notes that she lived separate from the other prisoners and refused to associate with them . . . she refused to allow others to use the only washbowl in the apartment (cell area), claiming that it was not conducive to a good complexion. With the scepter of the grand jury poised over her head and the very real possibility of a criminal indictment, "Mrs. Botkin is Boss." And, thus, we leave Cordelia Botkin secure in her pretentious attitude and turn to the grand jury, which would listen to the prosecutor's evidence and listen to the various witnesses. It would be their solemn duty in due course to decide her fate.

Chapter Seven

Strangest of All Cases Yields More Revelations

Concurrent to the legal battles which were being waged in the various courts and the ongoing search for the necessary physical clues, the police persevered in their probe for witnesses. These witnesses would be the persons who could testify to the veracity of the physical evidence. Upon them would fall the task of linking Cordelia to the crime and ultimately proving her guilt or innocence.

Some of these witnesses, such as the Delawareans, would provide the initial points of the case, which placed a connection to events in the East and led the investigation West. These witnesses, twelve in number, were of utmost importance, to the prosecution, for they furnished the foundation of factual evidence that a crime had occurred. Each was to provide a short deposition, which would yield the initial links in a chain of events, which would end at Cordelia Botkin's doorstep.

Other witnesses, specifically from San Francisco who had evidence, were necessary to offer the foundation of showing that Cordelia Botkin may have been the culprit in this infamous saga. These corroborating witnesses would offer affirmations before the grand jury and, included George Haas who provided confirmation regarding the source of the candy and the box. There was Frank Grey who identified Cordelia Botkin as the purchaser of arsenic.

Continuing the chain being forged by the prosecution were Sylvia Heney and Kittie Dettner, the clerks at the Haas Candy Store who sold the candy. Important also was Grace Harris, clerk at the City of Paris who was involved in the sale of the handkerchief. These witnesses and others, such as the postal officials, would provide the connection between the physical evidence and Cordelia and would justify the state's position.

Beyond these witnesses were the experts in handwriting and chemistry who would provide vital links to the circumstantial case with its mounting evidence. A surprise witness, David Green of Star Drugs, 1023 Market Street, would constitute an additional connection with respect to the prosecution's case regarding the arsenic. He would provide a link which would hopefully thwart one of the defense's contentions.

Most of the witnesses had been identified prior to the extradition attempts made by Delaware. Others would be located but say nothing until forced to by the grand jury, when the State of California made its decision to prosecute Cordelia. It was these witnesses, though some were not reluctant, who would provide a timeline of Cordelia Botkin's movements on dates prior to and following the detection of the murders. Their testimony would assist in piecing together the thought process and the actions of Cordelia Botkin preceding the crimes.

Of the multitude of persons that Cordelia Botkin consulted during her times of tribulation, there were two who stand far above the rest. We know, as fact, that Cordelia confided in her relatives and, in all probability, in her closest acquaintances; however, what they may or may not have known lies buried in the shadows of time. There were two persons to whom she spoke who were to provide evidence which, having been given in confidence, was not treated by either as such.

Neither it would seem appeared to be persons of a vengeful nature, though the defense would infer that they were later in the case. Both were performing in fact services for their employer. Each would provide "damning" evidence against Cordelia Botkin and show a side of her which had been quashed from public view. The women in question were Miss Lizzie Livernash (catchy name) of the *San Francisco Examiner* and Mrs. Almira Ruoff, Cordelia Botkin's nurse. Each was fortuitously placed at Cordelia's door in times of consternation and each was to provide damning testimony against her. It appears that neither sought the limelight. Livernash was performing a task in Healdsburg as an assignment for her employer, the *San Francisco Examiner.* Ruoff, as a nurse, was ministering to the needs of her patient Cordelia Botkin. Both through affidavits filed in the court and before the grand jury were cast into the limelight.

Miss Lizzie Livernash was instructed to conduct an interview with Cordelia Botkin in Healdsburg where she was a reporter. The date was August 16, and Cordelia's name had just surfaced in the investigation. In interviews during the next week, Lizzie was to gain knowledge of the travels of Cordelia Botkin around the time of the crimes. Ingratiating herself into Cordelia's confidence, she was able to attain facts concerning Cordelia's conduct during the period and provide police with one of the essentials for a person committing a crime—*motive.*

Synopsized here are the interviews as recorded by Miss Livernash and made available to the San Francisco authorities as they appeared in the *Delaware Gazette and State Journal*:

> . . . Mrs. Botkin was asked as to the alleged intimacy between herself and Dunning, the "lively" times at 927 Geary Street, and as to the truth of the statement said to have been made by her that no reconciliation would ever be effected between Dunning and herself.
>
> . . . Later Miss Livernash told Mrs. Botkin that she was under strong suspicion of having sent the poisoned candy to Mrs. Dunning. Mrs. Botkin became hysterical and exclaimed: "Oh, why didn't I let the man die! Better to have let the man die and spared the mother to her child." This reference to "letting the man die" is explained by the fact that she says she once saved Dunning from suicide.
>
> . . . On that journey she spoke of Mrs. Cordalay and of the firm friendship existing between the latter and Mrs. Dunning, "Mrs. Cordalay and myself are the most intimate friends the Dunning's have in San Francisco," said she. "She is a friend to the wife. I am a friend to the husband. Either she will be suspected of having sent that poison candy, or more likely it will be J (*Delaware Gazette and State Journal*, September 15, 1898).

In contrast to Miss Lizzie Livernash, Mrs. Almira Ruoff was in the best sense a reluctant witness. Early in the investigation, she had been contacted and stated from the outset, "I am not an intimate friend of Mrs. Botkin and do not wish to be, although I am sure she would wish me so" (*San Francisco Examiner*, August 26, 1898). She went on to say that she felt sympathy for her, but that Cordelia had placed herself in this precarious position and therefore it was none of her.

She denoted explicitly at the this time that she would not imply or evince any suggestion regarding the allegation as to whether Mrs. Botkin had purchased poisons nor would she comment on the intimacy between Mr. Dunning and Cordelia Botkin. Her feelings in this matter would be left until such time as she was summoned to appear before the grand jury.

It was clear that Almira had much to offer, but she revealed little. One thing that she did say was that she regretted the intimacy which did exist (or may have existed) between she and Mrs. Botkin. She, for her part, would not try to shield her in any way. Succinctly put, "I am not shielding Mrs. Botkin...I think it would be a great wrong if I did so. If she is guilty, I hope that she will pay for the terrible crime she has committed." (*San Francisco Examiner*, August 26, 1898).

When called, before the grand jury, she made a clean breast of all she knew. Parties unknown made veiled threats towards her, but she would not be deterred once her course was set. The family attempted to intimidate her by chastising her in the harshest terms. Mrs. Dora Brown, Cordelia's sister, composed the following communication and sent it to Almira Ruoff regarding her dear sister's case:

> Mrs. Ruoff:
>
> I little thought that you would use such an un-Christian spirit as you have in this case of my sister. It is, to say the least of it, unkind, and a mean, low act. I hope when I try to be a Christian I can forgive you–and you in my sister's (Mrs. McClure) house. **NOW LET ME SEE ANYTHING MORE FROM YOU AND I WILL ADVERTISE YOU AS AN INSANE ATTENDANT FROM THE ASYLUM.**
>
> Dora Brown
> (*San Francisco Examiner,*
> August 30, 1898)

Some might wonder if this was not inspired, or possibly composed, by Cordelia and then sent by sister Dora. The same haughty demeanor prevalent in Cordelia's speech can be seen within the prose. It has been a point of conjecture that a form of insanity was to be found in the Brown family. This, however, was not a point which was addressed in Cordelia's defense and, therefore, is a moot point.

Despite this tirade imposed by the Browns, Almira Ruoff became a star witness in the case for the prosecution. She was present during some of Cordelia's meetings with John Dunning and there would be through insinuation because of this question as to whether the relationship was more than just innocent friendship.

Almira Ruoff was also present ministering to Cordelia Botkin in July 1898 where the aforementioned was suffering from a cold (alleged pneumonia). Against Almira's wishes, Cordelia had summoned a physician, Dr. Thomas W. Stone, to care for her. During Dr. Stone's visit, in which he prescribed a small amount of opium, Cordelia queried him regarding the symptoms of *arsenic poisoning.* Good naturedly, the doctor suggested that strychnine would be a far better death agent. Also during the same sickness, Cordelia inquired to Almira as to two other important points. The first was when one purchased arsenic did the party have to give their name? Second did you have to give your name when you registered a piece of mail? Curious questions from a person who within weeks would be suspected of the murders of two women a continent away.

According to Mrs. Ruoff:

> She (Cordelia) is a clever actress, and I felt that she was such, a woman of many moods, indescribable, unfathomable, such is Mrs. Botkin. I neither could nor would repose confidence or trust in her . . . she is thoroughly selfish, caring not whom she may engulf or how much trouble and annoyance she causes others as long as her own ends are secure (*San Francisco Examiner,* August 31,1898).

Upon the facts of circumstantial evidence, thus far collected, the grand jury was asked to make its recommendation. These facts were based on not only the circumstantial, but also on the physical evidence and witness statements thus far secured. With two days of testimony completed, the foreman of the grand jury reported that their verdict was a True Bill. The indictment against Cordelia Botkin was affirmed on October 29, 1898.

The Indictment thus reported states:

> On or about August 12, 1898, in the State of California, Mrs. Botkin did, with malice aforethought, kill Elizabeth Dunning, by preparing certain candies containing poison "with the intent that the said candies should be eaten by the said Elizabeth Dunning, otherwise known as Mrs. John P. Dunning."
>
> It is further stated in the indictment that she mailed the package of candies in San Francisco, and that the same were delivered to Elizabeth Dunning in Dover, Delaware who ate them and died from the effects thereof. . . . No mention of Mrs. Deane's murder is made the Grand jury having decided it was sufficient to charge the murder of Mrs. Dunning (*The Call*, October 29,1898).

This matter was concluded on October 31, 1898. Cordelia Botkin was formally arraigned for the murder of Mrs. John P. Dunning, also known as Mary Elizabeth Dunning, in Judge Carroll Cook's court.

Chapter Eight

The Trial of Mrs. Botkin and the Useless Expenditure of State Funds

The stage was thus set for the next phase of the proceedings, the trial. It would gain national attention and be a conspicuous news feature in the waning months of 1898. On the 29th of October eastern newspapers, such as the *New York Daily Tribune* carried this communiqué.

> MRS. BOTKIN INDICTED FOR MURDER
> San Francisco, October 23–"The Chronicle" says that Mrs. Cordelia Botkin must stand trial here in the Superior Court on the charge of murder of Mrs. John P. Dunning, of Dover, Del. The Grand jury after a prolonged session has voted to indict her at five o'clock today; the indictment was presented to Judge Belcher (*New York Daily Tribune,* October 29, 1898).

Legal bickering between the prosecution, led by John A. Hosmer, and the defense, guided by George Knight, consumed the entire month of November 1898. Both sides, of the aisle, were jockeying for a favorable position in the trial, which was to follow and which would consume the entire month of December.

At the expense of the State of California, the Delaware witnesses were assembled and, with the exception of John P. Dunning who was in Chicago, began the onerous journey by train to San Francisco. The prosecution having divulged the entirety of its evidence through Chief Lees to the press and the community had few surprises left as the days abated till the beginning date of the judicial proceedings. From the prosecution's viewpoint there would be few opportunities for additional drama or anything of an astonishing nature.

Thereafter, it was left to George Knight and Frank McGowan to provide all the dramatic emphasis. It is a curious fact that neither of these attorneys ever grasped the enormity of the situation. From the point they were first engaged through the trial, neither of them ever mentioned that they believed in Cordelia's innocence. Instead of an immediate attack on the nature of the case, Knight and McGowan based their entire premise on the illegality of the State of California trying Cordelia Botkin. On more than one occasion, they made the ludicrous suggestion that there was no proof that Mary E. Dunning and her sister had died of arsenic poisoning. The two attorneys made light of the prosecution's circumstantial evidence and completely ignored the fact that a bona fide defense would be in the best interest of their client.

As jury selection commenced, the defense gave no indication of the direction it was prepared to travel. The indication was strongly suggested that George Knight was of the belief that he would be satisfied with any twelve impartial citizens who had not formed an opinion regarding the prosecution's evidence. The jury selection moved swiftly and within forty-eight hours of the trial's commencement, the twelve men chosen to judge Cordelia's fate had been selected. She, as both observer and defendant, expressed the greatest satisfaction at the progress of the contest. At the close of the second day, she was asked her opinion of the jury which had been procured from the long list of available talisman.

As in the past, Cordelia took center stage and launched into a spirited monologue.

> "I am perfectly content," she said "to leave my cause in the hands of these gentlemen. . . . I would have been satisfied with any twelve honorable citizens, who were not prejudiced against me as a consequence of the malicious falsehoods which have been published in the daily press. . . ."

She reiterated her innocence:

> . . . and then went one step further by stating . . . my consciousness of innocence has sustained me during my incarceration . . . I am thankful that my physical strength has been concomitant with my good spirits. Despite the lack of fresh air and the coarse fare of prison my health is excellent. . . . My attorneys have decided to give me an opportunity to refute the slanders against me, by placing me on the witness stand, when the proper time arrives . . . when this trial is over the world will know that I am free of guilt (*The Call*, December 8, 1898).

Was Cordelia delusional, or was she sincere in the supreme belief of her innocence? One can say that if nothing else, Cordelia was self-assured in her own thoughts concerning this question. With this said and the jury selection completed, Cordelia would, in fact, be placing her fate and life in the hands of twelve citizens not familiar to her or affected by her bombastic demeanor.

> *(To the Reader: It is noted from the outset that the case will not be presented in its entirety. For those who desire an in depth view, approximately 950 pages of transcript plus the additional appeals paperwork presented by the prosecution is available from the California State Archives.)*

The *State of California v. Cordelia Botkin* commenced on Friday, December 9, 1898, at 10:00 A.M. In his opening statement for the state, Assistant District Attorney John A. Hosmer laid the groundwork for the case which the state intended to prove during the prosecution of Cordelia Botkin. Step by step, Mr. Hosmer moved through the salient points showing the mitigating circumstances that by their logic would give credence to the state's suppositions. He concluded his opening remarks with the following: "Gentlemen, if we prove these facts we shall expect a verdict of murder in the first degree against the defendant." (*The Call*, December 9, 1898). With this completed, the State was ready to pursue its course and show the logic and chain of events, which though circumstantial assertions, would lead to a finding of guilt, on the part of Cordelia Botkin.

Expectations were high on December 10, 1898, for a quick and speedy trial. These hopes were soon dashed when an effort was made by W. L. Harper, a citizen and taxpayer assisted by a local attorney Louis P. Boardman, brought forth a petition to prevent the trial of Cordelia Botkin from taking place in California. The legal defenders of Mrs. Botkin had insinuated that they intended to spring a surprise on the prosecution and the debate soon raged. The crux of Mr. Harper's petition was that, as a taxpayer in the State of California, he and other Californians should not have the burden of the expense of this costly burdensome trial. It has been estimated that the prosecution of Cordelia Botkin would be in the neighborhood of $30,000.00 at its lowest, and Harper alleged that this was unjust and unwarranted.

Mr. Harper, representing the taxpayers of California, petitioned the Supreme Court for a Writ of Prohibition. It was hoped that through this Writ, Judge Carroll Cook and the Superior Court would be placed on notice. The price for justice was astronomical, and in light of this, it was hoped that they would cease the continuance of the trial. Louis P. Boardman who instituted the suit for his client was of the belief that he

> . . . had not been overzealous in the matter. I was prompted to a certain extent in what I have done by the manifest exigencies of the case as expressed by these gentlemen (Harper and unnamed friends) (*The Call,* December 11, 1898).

The Superior Court was clearly not amused by these frivolous shenanigans and set forth its own conclusions. These, in essence, being that the State did have a right to proceed under the Penal Code of 1872. If, in fact, the U. S. Supreme Court or the Supreme Court of California chose to take judicial notice, they were free to do so in their time but the case would proceed.

If Cordelia's attorneys were involved in any way, they quickly took a step backward to re-analyze their precarious position and to distance themselves from this impertinent act. It does, as has been said, bode well for an attorney who does not incur the wrath of a judge, especially during a legal proceeding. Charles Heggerty, speaking for the defense, discussed Harper's writ at length and chose his words wisely. He stated:

> "I feel morally certain that the Supreme Court will inform Attorney Boardman that there is nothing in the application whatever. I consider it a direct interference with the trial . . .

I believe it is trifling with the courts" (*The Call*, December 11, 1898).

The Superior Court agreed as any petition for any superfluous writ was to be set aside until the proceedings at hand were concluded. With Harper's petition addressed, court proceedings, which had been delayed, moved forward in earnest, and court readied itself to hear a recapitulation of the horrifying tale of the murders of Mary E. Dunning and Ida H. Deane.

Chapter Nine

When the Tale of Death Was Told Mrs. Botkin's Nerves Were Shaken

Without further opposition, the trial commenced on Tuesday, December 13, 1898, and the spectators who crowded the courtroom of Judge Carroll Cook would hear the macabre story of the poisoner's plot. Before the day was over, those present would be able to recite every facet of the beginnings of the assassin's scheme on August 9,1898. The gallery, the citizens, and the judge would be transported by word to the Pennington house in Dover and hear first hand the devastating facts as they had transpired on that morbid and lugubrious day. This was the beginning of the prosecution's attempt to weave the circumstantial web of evidence around Cordelia Botkin. Her name was never mentioned this day, but the intent and direction of the case was clear.

The prosecution's first witness was Thomas M. Gooden, postmaster of Dover, Delaware. Mr. Gooden was an excitable, nervous, person, but he was demonstrative concerning his recollections. Thomas Gooden testified as to the arrival of the package on the date in question, August 9. Mr. Gooden detailed the direction and the mode of travel from whence the package had arrived. He outlined the procedures within the post office itself and how the package came into his purview and hence into John B. Pennington's postal box, P.O. Box 335. Postmaster Gooden identified the package which was postmarked San Francisco and was addressed to "Mrs. John P. Dunning, Dover, Delewere."

Next to the witness stand was young Harry, who later changed his name to Henry C. Pennington, the grandson of John B. Pennington. The fourteen-year-old boy described how he came into possession of the package of death. He explained that, as was custom, it was his duty to go nightly to the post office and retrieve the family's daily mail from the postal box, a walk of three blocks. He relished with pride the trust that grandpa had for him. On the date in question there was in the box some letters and an oblong box. Harry retrieved the contents and retraced the three blocks to his grandfather's home.

When he arrived, the members of the family were seated as was custom following supper, on the front veranda of the house. Giving the box to his Aunt Elizabeth, he retired to the steps as a short discussion commenced concerning the origin of the box. The box, which he identified, was the same and was addressed to "Mrs. John P. Dunning, Dover, Delewere." Harry noted, under questioning, that when the box was opened it was found to contain candy, a small handkerchief and a note which read "Love to yourself and baby, Mrs. C."

The young lad stated that he partook of a piece of the candy as did other members of the family. He felt no ill effects until the next morning. Harry then detailed graphically his experience, which included a severe headache, vomiting, and an unquenchable thirst which lasted for a day and a half. The line of questioning undertaken during his cross-examination by George Knight, whether insightful or not, did offer at least a moment of comic relief.

Mr. Knight attained the knowledge that the Dover home was a large, roomy one. The Pennington's employed a colored cook and also a colored man who performed odd jobs. Regarding the evening meal, it was ascertained that it consisted of fish, corn fritters, and eggs. The suggestion was then intimated that there may have been trouble between Harry's grandfather and the cook Rosy. Answering all these assertions Harry maintained a gentleman like posture. Though pursued no further at this point, the insinuation had been made by George Knight and would be pursued in the future.

Following Harry to the witness box was his cousin Leila Deane, the fourteen-year-old daughter of Ida H. Deane. She identified the box of candy as the one received on the fateful night which set the course of events which removed her mother from her life. Leila stated it was hard to decipher the origin and acknowledged that she "read 'Francis' and that was all I could make out." Like Harry, she took some of the candy as the box was passed amongst the family. She explained that the next morning, she experienced dizziness, was languid, and had a desire to vomit. Leila stated that she had not thought about the cause of her illness and did not recover until sometime after her mother's death.

The third witness was Miss Josephine Bateman, a schoolteacher in Dover, dressed to the nines and possessing a demeanor perfectly matched to her occupation. With her testimony the prosecution cleared the air regarding any taint of the food or household. It was reported by the press that in one full swoop, "she cleared the cook, acquitted the fish, declared the corn fritters innocent, and re-established the spotless reputation of pots and pans." (*San Francisco Examiner,* December 13, 1898). She was a visitor to the Pennington home that fateful evening having stopped by after her evening repast. She had eaten of the candy but not of the supper.

She had seen the handkerchief and the note and had attempted because of her vocation to ascertain the address. Miss Bateman had sampled the offered treat, a cream chocolate with a pecan on top. Upon leaving the Pennington residence to resume her walk, she removed three lumps from her mouth and threw them to the pavement. Asked if she had suffered any ill effects from her encounter, Josephine Bateman responded that the next day her gums were ulcerated and she had pains in her stomach and felt nauseated and had the intense desire to vomit. Miss Bateman withstood a blistering examination by George Knight in which he posed numerous questions regarding her knowledge of arsenic. Mr. Knight was very happy to see that Josephine recalled the white substance to be in the form of lumps and not powder. The reasoning for this would be apparent as the trial progressed. That aside, Miss Bateman was indeed a good witness for the prosecution. She was always precise, explicit, and intelligent in her answers to all questions which were posed.

As the afternoon of the trial's first day progressed, the next witness was Miss Ethel Jane Millington. The daughter of George Millington, proprietor of the Millington (Capital) Hotel on the Green, she was young and blushing. Ethel related that she had accompanied Miss Bateman to the Pennington porch on the fatal evening of August 9, She related that she had partaken of the candy.

On the morning of August 10, Ethel had been nauseous and suffered a languid feeling throughout the day. Her recollections were similar to Josephine Bateman regarding the days which followed. Under cross-examination she stated that beyond this she had no other symptoms or disorders. There were no stomach pains or cramping, and she had no undo thirst. When the box of candy was placed before her, Ethel identified it and the contents: the candy, the handkerchief, and the note. The fish, fritters, cook, and pots and pans were further exonerated, by this young lady, as Ethel had not partaken of the evening meal at the Pennington house, either.

Joshua D. Deane was the next witness to be called to testify. Described as handsome though somewhat balding, Deane operated a stationery and cigar store on Loockerman Street in Dover. He was the husband of victim, Ida Henrietta. Under examination, Mr. Deane espoused in great detail the events which transpired in the aftermath of the candy delivery. Having eaten the supper, he had returned to his shop prior to the arrival of the candy. He thus put an end to the issue of poisoned fish or tainted corn. Graphically, he depicted the events of the late evening when his wife was taken ill. Deane related that the illness made his spouse very sick and that she continuously vomited and purged her body of the venom which had infested her person. Ida had related to him that she had severe pains in the stomach and she complained constantly that she was burning up with fever but was cold to the touch. He was extremely perplexed by the entire situation and remained closely at her side throughout the night.

Realizing that his wife was extremely ill, Joshua Deane had sent for Dr. Lemuel Bishop on the morning of August 10. With this physician, now in attendance, Deane placed himself in a secondary role alternately ministering to his wife and his daughter Leila. The end came Friday, August 11 in the early evening. Ida Henrietta's eyes suddenly became fixed and a pale, marble-like tone came over her skin. She convulsed once or twice, as he held her in his arms, and then she passed.

The defense in deference to the man, who had suffered such a grievous loss, asked few questions of him regarding his wife's death except to make rudimentary inquiries. Mr. Knight instead dwelt more on points concerning any suspicion the doctor may have regarding the mysterious package. Mr. Deane could offer little factual evidence concerning the events surrounding the package and with this attained, he was released from further testimony.

At the conclusion of the day, the bereaved father, John B. Pennington, was called to the witness stand. Seventy-three years of age, this tall, bearded gentleman, who was alert as a sentinel, had a very storied past. A lawyer since 1857, he had represented the State of Delaware in Congress from 1887 through 1891. He had at one time been the attorney-general for that state, and thus he was very seasoned in the ways of the law.

Mr. Pennington described the setting of the infamous crime which had claimed the lives of his two remaining children. He and his family lived in a charming old southern home, which was built in the Colonial style. The home fronted the Public Square and was capable of accommodating a large number of persons. With the preliminaries established he was asked about his son-in-law, John P. Dunning. The anxious crowd now was given its first glimpse of the man who was so intertwined with the course of events which had transpired and led to the untimely deaths. John Pennington stated that John Dunning had been admitted to the bar in Delaware some years previous. Mr. Dunning had not been enamored by his chosen profession and had drifted across country to San Francisco. He then pursued a career as an associate with the Associated Press, having served his apprenticeship in Wilmington as a journalist.

Matters next turned to the night of August 9, and he told of the supper and, as was his custom, of lying down in the parlor for approximately a half-hour to rest and digest. When he arose, he exited the house by way of the front porch to go to his office in the County Building directly across the Public Square. He related that present on the veranda were Mrs. Dunning, Mrs. Deane, Harry Pennington, Leila Deane, Elizabeth Dunning, Mrs. Pennington, and some others, presumably Josephine Bateman, Ethel Millington, and Ethel Clarke.

As he passed, John Pennington exchanged pleasantries with all present. and viewed Mary Elizabeth who was holding the box in her hand. She remarked to him, “See Papa, what a nice box of candy I have, and I do not know who sent it. Won’t you have a piece?” He declined, and pointed to his cheek. He had just placed a fresh plug of tobacco in his mouth and did not wish to spoil the taste. John Pennington then went about his business and returned sometime later to find the family playing Parcheesi.

Mr. Pennington discussed events which occurred later that night. He recalled hearing Ida Henrietta retching, of the illness of other members of the family, and the deaths of his two daughters.

He was shown the candy box and identified his initials JBP, which were clearly visible on the box. John Pennington explained that following Mrs. Deane's death, and shortly before Mary Elizabeth's, he had asked Mary the location of the box of candy. Mary though extremely ill had told him that she had placed it on top of the "secretary" in the back parlor.

After her death, he retrieved the package, and it was only then that he cursed himself for not being cognizant on the night of the package's arrival. The writing on the wrapper and the note inside were strangely familiar. He had seen such writing on two similar occasions. Mr. Pennington recalled letters which had arrived from San Francisco the previous summer. Mary Elizabeth had read the first and then showed it to him. She beseeched her father in no uncertain terms that should anymore letters arrive in this handwriting from San Francisco, he was not to show them to her. Though not vile in nature, the letter had a sense of foreboding.

John Pennington, ever the prosecuting attorney, adjourned to the County Building carrying the brown wrapper. Once there, he unlocked his desk and retrieved the additional two anonymous letters. To his untrained eye, the handwriting on all was ominously similar. Of greater interest, however, was the telling point, particularly that they had all been mailed in San Francisco. The mysterious package and its contents were maintained in his custody from this point, with the exception of five pieces of chocolate given to Dr. Bishop for transmittal to Dr. Theodore Wolfe for analysis. The evidence had left his possession only when it was delivered from his hand to Detective Bernard McVey.

Not much could be said by the defense, though George Knight did try. Once again he accused the cooking utensils as masterminding the heinous deed. In fact, at one point Knight even attempted to implicate the stove. Mr. Pennington, the consummate attorney, parried this insinuation and authoritatively brushed him aside with the emphatic response "No, we have been using them ever since."

Thus the day ended on an uncompromising note. The crime scene had been described and most of the Delaware witnesses had been examined. The next day would begin with the experts and accordingly lay the foundation for the prosecution's premise.

As the trial's second day began, a wearied Cordelia Botkin took her seat at the table occupied by her counselors. Hidden behind a black veil, her eyes were worn by the stress of the events which had so far transpired. The Delaware doctors, two physicians, and the state chemist would occupy the stage this day. The word "poison" would hang like a pallor over the courtroom as the physicians explained the course taken in the diagnosis and treatment of the victims, culminating in their deaths; the chemist would testify to his subsequent analysis of the candy.

Dr. Lemuel A. H. Bishop was the first to occupy the witness box. Under examination, he told of being called the morning of August 10 to attend the ailing sisters, Mrs. Dunning and Mrs. Deane. Dr. Bishop detailed the symptoms which he found and the medications prescribed from his initial contact with the victims until death finally overtook them. His early diagnosis was cholera morbus (food poisoning), but as time passed and neither of the patients showed improvement, he cast about for another source. It was then that arsenic poisoning came to his mind, for both ailments shared a number of common symptoms. On the morning of the 11th of August he had asked Dr. Presley Downes to enter the case as a consultant. After consultation the physician agreed that the victims exhibited all the symptoms of arsenical poisoning and because of the lapse in time and the progression of the poison, there was little hope of recovery.

Dr. Bishop revealed that subsequent to the two women's deaths, he had met with Mr. Pennington and had been shown the candy. He noted that he had requested of Mr. Pennington several pieces which he transmitted personally to Dr. T.R. Wolfe, a professor at the Delaware College, and who was also the state chemist for Delaware. The physician did well for the prosecution as a witness, but, as would soon be apparent, his testimony was on unsteady ground. Mr. Knight through his cross-examination had an unsettling effect upon the good doctor. Dr. Bishop attempted to side step the issues and deflect the attorney's questions. It became apparent to the packed courtroom that he had initially misdiagnosed the illness. The most damaging aspect brought forth by Mr. Knight was that "autopsies were not performed on either victim." This was, as Bishop was to admit, the only way to prove that Mrs. Dunning and Mrs. Deane had ingested arsenic.

Following Dr. Bishop to the witness stand was Dr. Presley S. Downes. He too, like Dr. Bishop, was a graduate of the University of Pennsylvania Medical School. Unlike Dr. Bishop, however, he was very sure of himself and gave short, concise, and positive testimony. His description of Mrs. Dunning's condition was a classic example of arsenical poisoning. The doctor summarized Mrs. Dunning's condition thusly. The patient was cold and clammy, face and body swollen, membranes of the nose and throat congested, eyes intolerant to light, heart weak, breathing labored, and intense burning sensations. After consulting with Dr. Bishop, he said at once, "This must be a case of arsenical poisoning."

Inroads previously gained by George Knight by his tortuous examination of Dr. Bishop had been dispelled. Try as he would, Mr. Knight could not shake nor rattle Dr. Downes. One positive stroke was gained from his testimony. It was elicited by the defense that Dr. Downes was not in complete agreement with Dr. Bishop's initial handling of the case and did have some reservations. He did agree with treatment given under the existing circumstances at the time of the consultation and afterward. Dr. Downes doubted that in the early stages any doctor would have detected the symptoms of arsenic poisoning and that by the time they exhibited themselves it was too late for the patients and any hope of convalescence would have been a miracle. His testimony concluded the day's morning session of court.

The court reconvened two hours after forenoon with the professor of chemistry at the University of Delaware and state chemist, Dr. Theodore R. Wolfe. Bearded and spectacled, Dr. Wolfe was the epitome of respectability. He explained in polysyllabic terms the analysis he had performed on five lumps of chocolate given to him by Dr. Bishop on August 15, 1898. His testimony was highly technical and, as it progressed, the teacher in him came to the forefront. Questioned by Judge Cook as to amount of arsenic he had found in his analysis, he responded "Eleven and one half grains." Inquiry was then made as to what would be termed a "lethal" dose. Dr. Wolfe responded that two to three grains would be sufficient to dispatch a normal person. In effect, the poison contained in the limited number of chocolates examined was enough to kill a horse.

It was obvious at this point that the poisoner had gone to great lengths to be certain of a killing. Dr. Wolfe's answer seemed to awaken Cordelia's interest and she stretched forward, across the defense table as if to say tell me more. George Knight made no attempt to attack the chemist's credibility. By innuendo, instead, Knight attempted to muddy the waters of Theodore Wolfe's damaging testimony. Mr. Knight curiously asked, if the chocolate appeared to have been cut and pasted together. He alluded to this fact that the poison could have been in the chocolate at the time of manufacture and was extremely interested in its composition. Dr. Wolfe advised that the arsenic was in the form of an amorphous form and that the powder was the result of attrition from larger pieces. This concluded the testimony of Dr. Wolfe, though he was to return in an attempt to resolve a controversy which was forthcoming.

The next three witnesses were minor in form and were presented at this point by the prosecution to show that the case had merit in the State of California and that the important custody of evidence had remained unbroken as it traversed the continent. These final three witnesses were Attorney-General Robert C. White, Delaware State Detective Bernard J. McVey, and Chief Lees of the San Francisco Police Department.

As the court prepared to recess for the day, word was received from the Supreme Court that the petition of W. L. Harper to prohibit Judge Cook from hearing the Botkin case had been refused. This issue was now put to rest and the case would proceed on its own merit.

Chapter Ten

Mrs. Botkin Wearied By the Long Tale of Death

The Delaware witnesses concluded the initial phase of the trial with the completion of their testimony. They had laid the groundwork for a positive outcome and had generally acquitted themselves well. Attorney-General Robert White was filled with pride and gives us a glimpse of this in the following telegram which he sent to George Millington regarding the case thus far:

> My Dear Millington: All the Delaware witnesses have testified, and to say I am proud of them would be putting it mildly. The little girls, Ethel Millington and Leila Deane were simply, out of sight. . . . They (the witnesses) have been complimented on all sides . . . they did themselves more than justice and Delaware is a much greater state in the estimation of California today than she ever has been before. . . . We have no doubt of conviction now. Our witnesses laid such a strong foundation that she cannot escape (*Every Evening,* December 20, 1898).

It would seem at the least in his mind that the outcome of the trial was without doubt as the scene shifted to the California witnesses. The coffin had been structured, and all that was left was to drive home the nails in the lid. December 15, 1898, dawned, hopefully, and with the commencement of court there was no inkling of the portent of disaster. Whereas the Delaware witnesses had been confident, almost self-assured, the prosecution, with the exception of two points, inexplicably found itself on shaky ground. Hopefully, the prosecutors sought to engender a positive stature from its first witnesses. Reluctantly, for the most part, they were forced to accept vacillation.

The first witness of the day was Professor Thomas Price, State Chemist of California. He was at odds with Professor Wolfe of Delaware from the outset of his testimony. Dr. Wolfe had found nothing but amorphous arsenic in his analysis, whereas Professor Price had found only crystalline, which was in total opposition. A raucous debate ensued between the two learned men who were at such a variance in their conclusions. During a brief recess both chemists once again analyzed the candies. This subsequent analysis brought a resolution to the debate; it was found that some of the pieces contained the amorphous variety in which there were no lumps. Others, upon examination, did in fact contain the crystalline variety. With these facts ascertained, the two scientists parted amicably and concluded that they both were correct in their previous assertions.

This caused some embarrassment to the prosecution, which had based its claim on certain fact. The defense showed no sign of surprise at this revelation. It appears that this well-guarded secret, which the prosecution attempted to suppress, had already come into their purview. As with today, sources within the police department, though unidentified had apparently leaked this pertinent information much to the chagrin of John Hosmer. For the most part, Professor Price's testimony was straightforward. Like Professor Wolfe, he presented his evidence without any confrontations from the defense which seemed contented with the paradoxical situation which had transpired. Dr. Price and Dr. Wolfe offered the groundwork for attestations which were to follow. Both scholars avowed that neither had "ever heard of arsenic being used as a bleaching agent." The witnesses who followed the chemist to the stand were for the most part mediocre. In their hands, unfortunately, the prosecutions case against Cordelia rested. There were bright spots, but with the witnesses this day, the thread of circumstance was frayed and stretched to the breaking point.

Frank Grey, the pharmacist at the Owl Drug Store, 1128 Market Street, set the course for the prosecution. His was the first of the testimony which was crucial to the advancement of the prosecution's theory and he was unflinching. As he took the witness stand Cordelia who had been outwardly calm and sedate began to stir with some agitation.

Mr. Grey testified that he had sold pulverized arsenic (powder) to a lady in June of this year. She had stated that her purpose was to use the poison to bleach a straw hat. He had questioned her regarding this and asked, if per chance, she would like another product which would be better suited. The lady was firm and replied forcefully that she had often used arsenic for this purpose and was very accustomed to it. At her insistence he measured and wrapped two ounces of the powder in paper and instructed her to follow him to the drug registry counter.

Druggist Grey, following the formality of the day, dutifully filled in the register. He wrote "Mrs. Botkin Victoria Hotel, California and Hyde Streets" When asked if the lady in question was present in the courtroom, Frank Grey without hesitation pointed to the defendant, Cordelia Botkin, as the lady who purchased the arsenic. All eyes turned to Cordelia and the courtroom buzzed with excitement. His identification was for the first time a direct implication directed that Mrs. Botkin had committed the criminal act.

The defense attempted to parry this blow by directly attacking Mr. Grey. He was badgered incessantly by George Knight. Questioned how he could be so sure that the lady was Cordelia Botkin, Mr. Grey stunned the courtroom. It was an easy question for him to answer. Frank Grey was positive in his identification because he knew Cordelia Botkin personally. He had met her on a number of occasions while he was working at the Baldwin Pharmacy in 1897. Mr. Grey had seen her since that time while working at the Owl Drug Store. The defense was rocked back on its heels but the damage had been done. Silence prevailed from their side and Frank Grey was released from further testimony.

Having made its first major inroad, the prosecution under the guidance of John A. Hosmer prepared to move forward. David Green, a pharmacist at the Star Drug Store, 1023 Market Street, was the next testifier to enter the witness box. Unfortunately, Mr. Green, who had boasted that he could assist the prosecution's case was not up to the task. Under examination by District Attorney Hosmer, David Green stated he had sold crystalline arsenic (lump) to a lady in May or June of 1898. Having established this point, the prosecution prepared to make its next telling point. Mr. Green was asked to whom he had sold the arsenic and how much. He replied that he had sold two ounces to a woman. When he was asked to identify the woman, he was not up to the occasion. David Green was definitely not a Frank Grey. The best that Mr. Green could say was that Cordelia Botkin was similar in appearance but as to whether she was the woman, his best response was "I could not answer." His testimony was anything but enlightening and bordered on disheartening.

David Green's testimony was a boomerang to the prosecution. John Hosmer was red with anger and rattled by this sudden change in events. Chief Lees and Investigator Gibson were left with the proverbial egg on their faces. A case which to this point had been concise, logical, and impregnable was beginning to teeter, as if at the edge of a precipice. In an attempt to regain its momentum and re-establish its course, the prosecution called its next witness to the stand.

This was the sales clerk from the George Haas Candy Store, 810 Market Street. Her name was Sylvia Heney and she can best be described as a slender wisp of a woman who was very shy in manner. Settling into the witness chair Sylvia commenced her testimony.

She described the events of the fateful Sunday, July 31 when she waited upon a strange and obnoxious woman. The customer had purchased a box of assorted chocolates in a one-pound box. She had told Miss Heney not to fill it, as there were additional items, she wished to add. Sylvia described the box with the words "Bon Bon" emblazoned on its top. She told of how she put ribbons at either end but could not recall if she added the Haas Candy seal. Assisted by Kittie Dettner, she had wrapped the box in plain brown paper and then handed the box to the woman. To Sylvia, the customer appeared nervous and to be in a hurry, as if she had a pressing engagement to attend. The following questions from the prosecution were crucial, but like David Green before her, she was not up to the task.

Asked to describe this customer, Sylvia stated she was not very tall and was rather stout. The prosecutor with all confidence asked Miss Heney if she could identify the woman. There was a pregnant pause. Sylvia was then asked, does the defendant resemble the person? The best the prosecutor could elicit from Sylvia Heney was "I think it is," which was delivered in a indecisive manner. Again, the prosecution and its witness had failed to live up to the expectations.

Following Sylvia Heney was her co-worker, Kittie Dettner, also present on that Sunday in July. With only a partial identification from Miss Heney, it was hoped that Miss Dettner could complete the link. If Kittie completed the identification, the prosecution would be back on course and sailing in a positive direction. Following the customary incidental questions, the questioning became more directed. Miss Dettner was positive in her assertions and thus collaborated Sylvia concerning the customer and candy purchase. She identified Cordelia Botkin from size, stature, and manner of pose but would go no further. This was far from a hanging identification, but it did give the jury cause for thought.

George Knight took the witness in hand and attempted to "peg away at her" but got little from his pains. He did get her to admit that attempts had been made by the police to suggest a positive identification, but beyond this he was stonewalled. Knight came close to committing that fatal error which many defense attorneys have committed. During the course of his examination, not content with what had been elicited, he came near coercing a more positive opinion from Kittie Dettner. This regarded the price paid for the box of candy which was purchased. Cordelia Botkin, true to form, felt she had to interject a suggestion regarding this question.

Quizzically, the jury and gallery must have looked at her incredulously. If she was not the lady who purchased the candy, why was she so concerned? It was as reported by the San Francisco Examiner "the case of . . . a parrot who talked too much." George Knight attempted to cover this blunder and terminated his cross-examination, thus concluding testimony for the day. Having been thwarted in its endeavor to produce a positive impact on the jury, the prosecution began, once again to weave the chain of fact, which would prove its circumstantial case. It had made some inroads, but the effects had been thwarted by a stubborn, unyielding defense.

As court reconvened this day, the murmuring in spectator's gallery was incessant. John Dunning, the star witness for the prosecution, was to make his appearance. Men and women jockeyed for position and fought to gain entry into the packed courtroom of Judge Cook. All eyes were turned to Cordelia Botkin as she arrived and took her seat followed by her entourage. It was noticed that on this day her demeanor had changed. Whereas previously she had been withdrawn, reclusive, and sedate, today in the language of the pavement, Mrs. Botkin was "getting gay." On this day she was bouncing, chatty, and peculiarly alive. Odd for a person suspended from the scales of justice and perched between life and death.

The day began with G. F. C. Droge, the manager of the George Haas Candy Store. A mundane creature, Droge did little to assist the prosecution. Mr. Droge's only positive moment was that he confirmed the fact that Sylvia Henry was employed at Haas on July 31 and was working as a counter person. He affirmed that he had witnessed the candy sale, but alas the old man was not sure if the purchaser was a man or a woman. His testimony complete, Mr. Droge was released from further inquiry.

Once again, George Knight attacked the "pots and pans." He insinuated that the arsenic might have formed in the copper kettle, the marble slab, or perhaps, it was in the condensed milk. Mr. Knight attacked the glucose, coloring matter, and other ingredients used in the candy making process. It appeared that nothing would escape his eye. Like the cook in Delaware who prepared the evening meal, he theorized perhaps there was a disgruntled former employee at the Haas Company who may have had a vendetta. Unscrupulously George Knight even attacked, "Rough and Rat," the company cat, as the arsenic inducer. Fortunately for the prosecution, Mr. Henry J. Pape, foreman at the candy company, testified next, and he cleared all the would be conspirators including the cat.

The following witnesses included George W. Haas and all the employees of the Haas Candy Company. Mr. Haas was forced to divulge all in his testimony regarding the candy making process. Through George Haas and the employees, all the secrets of his candy making process which had been secret were now public knowledge. Little if anything was gained through their testimony; however, the case plodded forward. Both the gallery and the jury sighed in a sense of collective relief as the last of the Haas Candy Company exited the witness box.

With the next witness, Mrs. Loretta Simpson, former landlady of the Victoria Hotel, the scene changed. She had been the proprietress of the hotel during the time when Cordelia and John P. had shared a residence. Expectantly, the gathered throng anticipated the sordid details of their adulterous relationship. They were sadly disappointed, for beyond the fact that she was aware of their cohabitation, Mrs. Simpson offered few details of substance. She had been present when the telegram assigning Dunning to a post in Cuba had arrived, and Simpson detailed numerous conversations with Cordelia regarding Mrs. Botkin's fear that John P. would be injured or killed in that far away place. She stated that during her tenure and theirs she had never witnessed any improprieties.

Loretta Simpson was a perfect example of the Victorian Age. With the exception of offering the route of the cable car line, which would have placed Cordelia Botkin in the immediate vicinity of the candy store and the druggist establishment, Loretta was the model witness for the defense, rather than the prosecution.

An inspector from the United States Post Office, James W. Erwin, was next summoned to testify. His was a rather dull and routine testimony, as he related post office procedures and various routes. Shown the wrapper from the candy box, Erwin testified that it did carry a San Francisco postmark, but as to its point of origin, there was no clue. The box could have been placed in the mail at any location within the city. James Erwin was a consummate professional and espoused that the package would have been marked at the Ferry Station. All mail leaving the city was stamped at this point, and it was impossible to ascertain from which substation it had come. He concluded his testimony by confirming that a package mailed August 4 from San Francisco would have arrived in Dover, Delaware, on the evening of August 9.

The only drama of the day occurred with the calling of the next witness. To this point the testimony had been dawdling and wearisome. Suddenly, the clerk of the court uttered, "John P. Dunning." Excitement spread through the courtroom in one long expectant gasp as all present came alive with anticipation. The bailiff joining in the excitement bounded to the witness room. As John P. Dunning exited the room and moved toward the witness box, one could feel the excitement in the air. Cordelia and he exchanged a momentary glance as their eyes met and a look of pain came over her countenance. Without warning John Dunning was taken by the arm and as the crowd sat in stunned silence, he was escorted back to the witness room. Was he in danger? Had he been threatened? The answer to both questions was no.

There appeared to have been a mistake and when it was made known, all anxiety ceased. The prosecution had called as its next witness, John B. Dunnigan and not John P. Dunning. This was the error. Amazingly there were two men with nearly the same name and both were witnesses on the same court docket. John B. Dunnigan, mail clerk at the Ferry Post Office, now dutifully, proceeded to the witness box. With his testimony, the prosecution was to secure the necessary link between the "mysterious package" mailed from San Francisco and received in Dover, Delaware. He admitted that through the course of a day he processed a multitude of packages. However, this unobtrusive oblong box had caught his attention. The box was addressed to John P. Dunning, Dover, Delaware. As the name was so similar to his own, he commented upon it as he postmarked it for its final destination. Mr. Dunnigan recalled not whether Mr. or Mrs. proceeded the name, but his testimony was a telling point.

Having released John Dunnigan from further examination, the case turned back to the Victoria Hotel and the evidence which would further strengthen the prosecution's premise. The present proprietress of the Victoria Hotel, Mrs. Birdie Price, was called next to the stand. Her testimony was important to the prosecution's contention that Cordelia Botkin did have an opportunity to commit the heinous deed. Birdie's deposing included facts relating to the movements of Cordelia on the fateful day of July 31. Mrs. Price testified that Cordelia had complained of illness and wished her meals to be served in her room. Believing the assumption that Mrs. Botkin was ill, Birdie Price complied. She was surprised, therefore, later in the day to see Cordelia with packages entering the Victoria Hotel shortly after the Haas Candy girls had said she purchased chocolates. Birdie Price was firm in her belief that Cordelia was fully dressed and was carrying packages. Unfortunately, she could not fix an exact time to the date. For the benefit of the defense, she did state that following Cordelia Botkin's departure, her rooms at the Victoria Hotel had been rented to several people. This placated Mr. Knight and brought a degree of doubt to the State's final witnesses of the day.

The area of testimony which brought closure to the day's proceedings centered on the infamous candy seal from a George Haas Candy box. Called as a witness was William Rosello who spoke on the subject of his rental of room number 26, previously occupied by Cordelia Botkin. Both he and the last witness of the day, W. W. Barnes, a clerk at the Victoria Hotel, testified to the gold seal partially obstructed from view by a carpet and sofa.

Because their testimony was adverse to the defense, Mr. Knight attacked the credibility of their statements with vehemence. He assaulted Mr. Rosello with a vengeance accusing him of being a police "dummy" (a plant). He next questioned the veracity of Mr. Barnes and accused the witness of more than employer-employee relations with Mrs. Price. This was done, as defense attorneys oft do, to cast doubt on a witness's credibility and to steer the jury from what on its face was damning testimony.

After Mr. Knight concluded, the jury was released for the day and the court was adjourned. Methodically, the prosecution had begun to move forward again in a positive manner endeavoring to reassert itself. Intertwining the mediocre with the self-assured, it began to tighten the web, like the ever patient spider, around Cordelia Botkin. The last day of the testimony for this week would see but three witnesses.

Chapter Eleven

Crowding Mrs. Botkin Toward the Death-Trap or to a Life of Sorrow Within a Felon's Cell

As court reconvened, Mr. D. Eklund was summoned to the witness stand. The previous day's supposition by the defense was that a disgruntled former employee may have been responsible for placing the arsenic in the chocolates, and he/she may have been the villain, not Cordelia Botkin. Mr. Eklund was a candy maker who had left employment with the George Haas Candy Company and soon dispelled another of George Knight's red herrings. He had, as he explained, left his employer for no other reason than he was suffering from ill health. Mr. Eklund denied emphatically ever putting arsenic or any other poison in chocolate. Having been parried by the prosecution, George Knight sat by idly and fumed.

Mrs. Grace Harris was the next witness to be called to the witness box. Cool, well poised, clear and concise, she was to prove a formidable witness for the prosecution. She was sworn and then struck a graceful attitude, surveying the courtroom before bringing her eyes into direct contact with Cordelia. So intent was she that Cordelia who had returned her gaze was for once unnerved and forced to look away.

In answer to perfunctory questioning, Grace Harris stated she had at one time been employed by the City of Paris. As the assembled mass within the courtroom looked on, Grace Harris, the saleswoman, as she preferred to be called, settled down to the task at hand. John Hosmer fumbled with evidence in a sluggish but deliberate fashion. He tantalized the gallery. Finally, opening an envelope he produced the small lacy handkerchief. Asked if she could identify the object in front of her, Grace Harris scrutinized it. Choosing her words carefully, she stated that the handkerchief came from the City of Paris, in fact from her department. She recognized the fabric, but in addition, identified the price mark as the store's. The City of Paris, of all stores in San Francisco, was the only one to use this type of mark.

With the identification in hand, the Prosecutor moved slowly and deliberately onward. Questions ranged from "how long the item had been on sale in the store?" to "have you ever sold a handkerchief of this nature?" Mrs. Harris gave a positive response to both. Mr. Hosmer was setting the stage, and one could sense the drama which was about to unfold. Cordelia sensed the danger which was forthcoming, and as Grace Harris looked upon her again, she became unsettled, fanning herself profusely and fidgeting in her chair. Mrs. Harris was asked if she had sold such a handkerchief to a lady, she responded that she had sold two to the same person. She was questioned further as to whether this person had given an address. Her response was dramatic: "yes, The Victoria Hotel."

As Mrs. Harris continued to testify the atmosphere within the courtroom became evermore agitated; everyone present waited with bated breath. She was asked if she had ever seen the defendant before. Her answer was perplexing as she said, "Yes, the first day of the trial." John Hosmer was not content with this answer and in a more persisting tone, asked the question again. To this Grace Harris answered that "She resembles the lady I sold the handkerchief too." The "coix de grace" had been executed; the gauntlet thrown down. Cordelia Botkin closed her eyes, bit her upper lip, and slumped in the chair. She attempted to show grit as she regained her composure, but it was all for naught.

With this completed George Knight attempted to salvage something, even a small piece from the moment. He attacked Grace Harris with the same remorseless, vindictive remarks that had caused Loretta Simpson and Birdie Price to whimper and cringe in fright. Mrs. Harris was not a woman torn from the same cloth, and Mr. Knight's intimidations this day would not succeed. She freely admitted that by waiting on the defendant, she had committed an indiscretion. Grace Harris acknowledged that there was a firm policy within the store regarding customers, and that she had waited on Cordelia Botkin out of turn. Within the City of Paris, this was tantamount to a flogging offense. She also acquiesced that the billing slip to the Victoria Hotel had gone missing, but beyond this she did not retreat.

Pressing forward, George Knight felt he was making some inroads into this stubborn woman's testimony. Mr. Knight, however, forgot the first tenet of an attorney. The tenet is that one should never over-try a case. And with the next question from his mouth, he imbedded another nail in Mrs. Botkin's coffin lid. He asked Mrs. Harris with a tinge of sarcasm, "Now, because you had broken one of the rules of the house Mrs. Botkin impressed you, was that all?" A stunned silence followed as Grace Harris replied "No, it was because of her resemblance to one of my dead relatives." In all stupidity, George Knight, the consummate professional, the defender of the down-trodden, asked "Who did she resemble?" Without batting an eye Grace Harris replied, simply, "My Mother." (*San Francisco Examiner,* December 17, 1898).

As the words were spoken, Mr. Knight realized he had gone too far. Grace Harris could have picked this woman from a crowd of thousands, for a woman has that ability, especially if one resembles her mother. George Knight had tried to bite, chip, and chisel at Grace's testimony, but on this occasion, he was the one bitten, and he was bitten hard. With a few further questions, he attempted to undo the damage he had created, but with little success. George Knight had succeeded where the prosecution had failed. He had elicited the elusive, positive identification of Cordelia Botkin and confirmed the testimony of so many indecisive witnesses.

The final witness for the day, as it was to be a short day, was another person with the potential to destroy Cordelia Botkin. She was, as the papers were to report, the day's delight–Mrs. Almira Ruoff. She had said early in the investigation that she would be a reluctant witness due to her close association with Cordelia's other sister, Mrs. McClure. If called to present testimony, however, she would tell all and she was true to her word.

Still blistering after the self-imposed damage done by the previous witness, George Knight prepared himself for the onslaught of a person who coursed pure venom from her lips. A Christian at heart, this did not sway Almira Ruoff from being present at the debauchery that took place between Cordelia and John P. Almira was present during many of the romantic moments, the drinking of the whiskey, and the aftermath.

Reluctant as she was, Almira Ruoff was of that pious variety of souls who can hide nothing from the Lord and would, as the wags were to say, be the first woman at a hanging to pull the rope. She freely admitted to being, in the City of Paris, with Cordelia Botkin and noted, when shown the handkerchief that it was of the same nature as one which Cordelia had shown her. Cordelia had purchased none on that date but she had noted that they were on sale and she intended to have one.

The infamous letters of 1897 to Mary Elizabeth in Dover, Delaware, were introduced into evidence as was the letter to Governor Budd requesting assistance for Cordelia going to Cuba as a nurse. The first letter, dated San Francisco, June 17, 1897, was read in full to the Court and beyond capacity gallery:

> Mrs. Dunning: My dear madam, will you please pardon the presumption the following information will disclose as I am a friend of yours and considering you have been greatly wronged is my sole object of doing this. Your husband's financial difficulties this last winter were not all due by any means to race track speculations. He has been all winter very closely associated with a lady that has a great influence over him, in fact they have been greatly together for a year and a half. Many person know of his being most constantly with her at the race track and theatres, that they have had apartments together can be proved to you. I don't know to what extent she caused his involved financial condition; they both were given to drink; he has forfeited all right to your confidence and all your friends think the same; I suppose you know he has left the city and might be with you even now as far as I know. Now, I hope you will take this as it is meant. I consider you have been greatly wronged in every way. This woman is quite clever and was very good to him and is divorced from her husband. With kind consideration and the sympathies of a woman, I am ever your friend, one that you would know (Transcript of Appeal, Criminal No. 632, February 1900, People's Exhibit 22).

Next, the prosecutor introduced the second letter dated San Francisco, July 10, 1897:

Mrs. Dunning: I sincerely hope that you have made all due inquiry concerning the grave information I send you out of the pure interests I have in you concerning the conduct of your husband, and if you have not you are not the woman I always supposed you were; if you would ever renew your former living with a man after so forgetting you as he did and place you in the position he so premeditatedly did. All you require to be convinced is to ask of many of both yours and my own friends that from the hour you left to go to your home after he returned from a trip to Los Angeles he was constantly with this interesting and pretty woman, who, by the way, is an English woman. She is now divorced from her husband, all owing to the marked intimacy with Mr. Dunning. Her husband is now free from her, and your husband was to co-respondent to the case. She was somewhat of an English income and is interesting in many ways to a degree. I am now in possession of the knowledge that Mr. D. is not with you and do hope your womanliness will prevent you ever being so again. Now don't misunderstand me concerning my saying of this woman; she is and was a lady by birth and education and when on the other hand they both of them lived in the extreme delights of a quiet Bohemian life. You can make all the inquiries you want as to the address as I gave you. They live at all the stores in that neighborhood, and the manner they live, which was 927 Geary Street, as they went in and out of there at all hours of the day and night. I think she does not live here now; I think in some place south of this State. I am sure you ought to ask; if you are not satisfied even the gentlemen that now has the position in your husband's place will tell you all you would want to know, and by all that is just in this life to you that position ought to be now held by Mr. D., for his dissipation morally and through drink had placed himself and his family where they are. He would never have left the wom. for you or your child. It was her advice no doubt when there was no more money to squander. This is all for your sake, so kindly take it as intended. Your friend (Transcript of Appeal, Criminal No. 32, February 1900, People's Exhibit 20).

Concluding the letter submissions, Mr. Hosmer introduced into evidence the letter to Governor Budd, San Francisco, April 18, 1898:

> Governor Budd–Dear Sir: Will you kindly grant my sincere request, which is to be placed on the nurse staff. It will be my heartfelt wish to render all the care and sympathy that such a position would demand. My reference in the city is Dr. Thorn. Trusting my request will receive an early response, I am, most respectfully, Mrs. W. A. Botkin, 1105 Hyde Street (Transcript of Appeal Criminal No. 632, February 1900, People's Exhibit 18).

As the letters were introduced, Almira Ruoff was asked if she had sufficient knowledge of Cordelia Botkin's handwriting to identify it. Without hesitation, the witness stated "I would know it to the antipodes." (*San Francisco Examiner*, December 17, 1898).

If not already a direct accusation, Almira Ruoff had sufficient courage to go further into the matter. Regarding the July 17 letter, she stated there were expressions which she had heard Cordelia Botkin use. If nothing else, the term, "Bohemian life" was to her a dead give away. It was, as Almira Ruoff testified, one of Cordelia's favorite expressions. If this was not a sufficient condemnation of Cordelia Botkin as a murderess, Almira's next assertions were the icing on the cake. Testimony soon left letters behind and the prosecution's course pursued another direction. This concerned the use of poison.

Cordelia, according to Mrs. Ruoff, had asked if she had ever been troubled by rats and, if so, what was the poison to eradicate them. Almira had informed her that strychnine was a useful agent. Pondering the answer, Cordelia had inquired if arsenic could be used as a viable substitute? The subject next turned to postage on packages. When questioned as to why, Cordelia had stated she was thinking of sending one. Almira, after determining the weight, which was approximately one pound, suggested that she send it registered. Her reasoning was as registered mail the postal authorities would not open it.

As Cordelia's friend and private nurse, Almira Ruoff, was indeed a wealth of potentially damaging information. Without hesitation and without prompting, she expounded upon a variety of incidents which had occurred in the period just prior to the murders. Almira explained how Cordelia at the time or shortly after the poison questions had asked a rather paradoxical question. This related to doctors and lawyers. Cordelia had asked, "If a person was in trouble and should employ a lawyer or a doctor would it be necessary to tell them everything?"

She spoke of a meeting under questioning, between Cordelia and Welcome A. Botkin in Stockton. Cordelia had been extremely agitated as they entrained from San Francisco. Heated words were exchanged between Cordelia and Welcome once they had arrived in Stockton. Listening from the hallway of the hotel where she was asked to remain, Almira had heard most of the conversation. As the two, Cordelia and Almira, left, the former remarked that she and "the governor," referencing Welcome A., had arrived at an understanding.

Shortly after this meeting, Cordelia summoned Almira and stated she believed she had contracted pneumonia. As a registered nurse, Almira Ruoff attempted to placate her but to no avail. As instructed she contacted a local physician, Dr. T. A. Stone, who responded to Mrs. McClure's residence, where they were staying while in Stockton. After a short examination he medicated her slightly and said he would return.

Recovery apparently was instantaneous, almost miraculous. When the good doctor made his visitation the following day, Cordelia was in good spirits. She immediately engaged him in conversation in regards to the different types of poison available. She was specific as to types, what their effects were, and how they reacted in the human system. Almira stated that thinking the worst, she advised the doctor not to tell her anything (Apparently, Almira feared that Cordelia had intentions of harming herself).

Dr. Stone, however, took it as a joke and expounded upon the virtues and drawbacks. Cordelia pressed him for answers regarding strychnine and arsenic. He responded lightly that strychnine was too harsh and the side effects for a person intending suicide were repulsive. Of the two, arsenic would be the poison of choice. Thereafter they engaged in a drawn out conversation about arsenic until Cordelia had received information concerning all the whys and wherefores.

Soon after this, Almira and Cordelia had parted company and came not again together until the 18th of August. At this time accompanied by Miss Lizzie Livernash, *San Francisco Examiner* reporter, she had arrived unannounced at Mrs. Ruoff's residence.

After the compensatory introductions, Miss Livernash was excused from the room. Cordelia at once launched into a deep monologue concerning the conversations with Dr. Stone in Stockton. Upon being informed that Almira recalled all of the collateral events, Cordelia went into hysterics. A doctor was summoned to assist her in regaining a semblance of composure. Questioned by Almira as to her demeanor, Cordelia offered the fact that she had told Miss Livernash about certain anonymous letters which she herself had received. It was at this point that Almira said Cordelia made her initial statements against those who wished to put her out of the picture.

Almira spoke frankly to Cordelia on this date and told her to go to the papers. Her feeling, she said, was if you have done nothing wrong, you have nothing to fear. The testimony of Almira Ruoff was like something from a Shakespearean tragedy. The ramifications stemming from her knowledge were beyond Almira's scope in life. Instead of keeping her countenance to herself, Cordelia had placed Almira in the position of her chief accuser and Almira Ruoff now hung above her head like the "Sword of Damocles."

With this knowledge attained, the prosecution turned once again to the question of arsenic. Almira said that in May a conversation had taken place at the Victoria Hotel. Cordelia had asked Almira about her previous profession which was in millinery. On its face the question Cordelia asked next was innocent. Had Almira ever used arsenic in the process of bleaching hats? Mrs. Ruoff stated in all her years she had never heard of arsenic used in that manner. Cordelia stated that she had heard from reliable sources that arsenic was good for the purpose. Her questioning on the subject next turned to the method of acquiring arsenic. Almira advised that all that was required was to state your purpose to any good chemist, and a person would have no trouble making the purchase.

Almira Ruoff was, at this point, turned over to Mr. Knight by John A. Hosmer, who stated simply, "Take the Witness." Once burnt, George Knight appeared to have been unready to do battle with this formidable opponent. He made cursory interrogatories but settled on a more course approach. Rather than attempting to impeach this witness, he chose to insult her. His most prominent question to Almira was "How long were you in the asylum?" It was Mr. Knight's endeavor to leave the jury with the premise that at some time Almira Ruoff had been institutionalized. The truth was that during her career she had been a nurse caring for the clinically insane. With but a few brief questions the witness was released, and the damage caused by her testimony was left to the jury to decide.

With this the day was concluded as the next witness, Miss Lizzie Livernash, was unavailable until Monday. She had been mentioned during Ruoff's testimony, but the extent of her testimony was unknown. Court was recessed for the weekend and all on the defense side sighed in relief, except for Cordelia. Mrs. Botkin, true to form, felt that she must have the last word. The *San Francisco Examiner,* December 17, 1898, printed the following statement:

> I knew from the affidavit Mrs. Ruoff made to the police what the substance of her evidence would be, so what she said on the stand did not surprise me in the least. Mrs. Ruoff has long been on friendly terms with me; she has accepted our hospitality and–well, I do not want to criticize the woman or to cast any reflections on her actions. She has given her testimony, and when my turn comes I shall do the same. For I have resolved to take the stand in my own behalf, and my attorney's offer no opposition to this course. What I shall say will clear away many of the misleading statements that have been made. I wish to take the stand, that I may have the opportunity of telling the story and presenting the facts of this matter in a way that will be comprehensible to all intelligent men and women. It is my intention, when I go into this matter, to tell the entire story; to hold nothing back. For it is only by a thorough explanation that this matter can be properly sifted and correct results obtained. As for Mrs. Ruoff, I shall not give her any serious consideration, for what she has said will in no way affect my peace of mind. It would, of course, if I were not able to explain and refute. To-day was Mrs. Ruoff's day in court. After a while, in a few days, things will assume a very different aspect.

Chapter Twelve

Dunning Sent to Jail for Refusing to Answer a Question

The trial was progressing rapidly and drawing near to its end. Both the prosecution and the defense professed satisfaction with its course thus far. For the defense, the weekend was spent in rapt anticipation as they prepared to meet the onslaught of the final witnesses for the State.

There would be but two witnesses for the prosecution as court commenced on Monday, December 19. Miss Lizzie Livernash and John P. Dunning. The day would be shortened as one of the jurors, Abe Jacobs, had suffered a death in the family. Court was recessed to reconvene at two P.M. and with the tolling of the two o'clock bell, the gallery, packed to capacity, murmured with anticipation.

Miss Lizzie Livernash, a *San Francisco Examiner* reporter, was summoned to the witness box. Having ingratiated herself upon Cordelia Botkin shortly after the murder, she had much to tell. Lizzie Livernash was indeed a force with which to be reckoned. She was quick and sharp of speech, showed extreme confidence, and was positive in manner.

As a confidant and as an eavesdropper, the facts which she possessed were devastating to the defense. She related that she lived in Healdsburg and had been directed by the *San Francisco Examiner* to go to the McClure home on August 15 and interview Mrs. Botkin. This first meeting with Cordelia resulted in the insinuation that the lady may have had some knowledge of the Dover murders. Asked by Miss Livernash if she had any idea as to the persons who poisoned Mrs. Dunning, Cordelia said she had not. Cordelia described Mrs. Dunning as a woman with many friends and no enemies. It was at this time that Cordelia intimated that the poisoned candy might have been sent by a friend who did not know it was in the candy.

They spoke again the next day and Cordelia's demeanor had seemingly changed. She advised Lizzie Livernash that if she, (Cordelia), were speaking for publication, she should first consult a lawyer. Lizzie Livernash agreed and told Cordelia that it was a wise decision if she was involved in the tragedy. Denying any complicity in the act, Cordelia launched into a detailed monologue of her association with Mr. Dunning. She told of how they met and then went into the specifics of their relationship. Cordelia spoke of the financial distress Dunning had brought on himself through gambling, the race track, and drink. Cordelia had kept John Dunning both monetarily and emotionally, and thus felt she had saved him from committing suicide.

Lizzie stated the two spoke the following day, and it was during this conversation that she indicated to Cordelia for the first time that there was talk and suspicion that she had committed the crime. She described the expression of shock that came over Cordelia and how she had become hysterical. With a horrified look followed by a distressful moan, Cordelia exclaimed, "Oh, why didn't I leave the man to die? I should have saved the wife and child" (*San Francisco Call*, December 20, 1898).

Regaining her composure somewhat, a decision was made that the next day Cordelia would travel to Stockton to seek the aid and advice of her husband, Welcome A. Botkin. Lizzie Livernash, the consummate professional, offered to travel with Cordelia as a companion. It was indeed an enlightening experience for Lizzie, as Cordelia spoke freely during the venture. One discussion which ensued regarded the telegram sent by Mr. Pennington to California, which pointed a finger of suspicion at Cordelia.

The lady was much distressed by this intimation. She felt that if John Dunning read this condemnation, he surely would blow out his brains. Cordelia expounded upon the criminality of the events and ventured the supposition that some unknown enemies had forged handwriting in the candy note. Prattling on Cordelia spoke of poisons and speculated that their inclusion in the candies may have been accidental. Mrs. Corbalay's name once again entered into the fray as a person who may have had a motivation to implicate Cordelia due to some unexplained vendetta.

For Lizzie Livernash, it was not an uninteresting train excursion; in fact, as some news people would say it was a reporter's delight. With little prodding, Lizzie was witness to a woman filled with nervous energy. This woman, companion if you like, appeared to have a need to direct all attention away from herself and onto the heads of others. Mrs. Corbalay was but one of a number of women who Cordelia charged with the crimes. In quick succession, she implicated Mrs. Seeley, Mrs. Arbogast, and Mrs. Forcade. From Cordelia's view, all had stronger reasons to be suspected than herself.

Arriving in Stockton, the ladies took rooms at the Imperial Hotel where they were to meet Mr. Botkin. Having exchanged cordialities with Lizzie, Mr. Botkin requested that he and Cordelia be left alone. Waiting in the hallway, Miss Livernash was privy to the entire conversation. Cordelia, with great excitement and in loud tones, pleaded with Welcome A. to save her. Sensing that her chortling was falling on deaf ears, Cordelia began to threaten her husband and "that woman" with exposure if he did not aid her in this time of need. Finally, as if to placate her and to save himself from further badgering, Welcome A. acquiesced. Cordelia was indeed a woman of extremes who had no fear of "removing the gloves" in order to get her way.

It was shortly after this meeting of the minds and during a brief interview between Lizzie and Cordelia that Beverly Botkin, Cordelia's son, made his presence known. Seriously intoxicated, Beverly began cursing reporters and suggesting he would like to send them all to the depths of hell. Attempting to pacify his anger, Cordelia chastised her son for the intrusion and begged him to not make a scene.

At this point, he was asked by Lizzie Livernash about John Dunning and about the gentleman's relationship with the young man's mother. In conversation, Beverly made certain remarks about Jack Dunning's love for his mother and Cordelia stated, in a rush of excitement, " . . . my son has the power to damn me." Having elicited this point of questionable evidentiary value, John Hosmer concluded his examination and Miss Livernash was given over to Mr. Knight for his cross-examination.

Realizing these revelations had a great impact on his case, George Knight attacked Lizzie Livernash with savage vigor. Lizzie

Livernash's testimony had placed his client in dire straits, and it appears he was convinced the case had reached a desperate point. To her credit, despite the personal attacks she was forced to endure, Lizzie Livernash stood firm. Knight made minor inroads into her testimony, but she sustained, for the most part, her credibility. George Knight, to his personal discredit and to the California Bar as a whole, conducted himself in a disgraceful and undignified manner. Having embarrassed California and its legal ethics, Knight released Lizzie from further examination.

The last witness for the day had been long awaited and was eagerly anticipated by the throng in the gallery. John P. Dunning entered the courtroom from the witness room and proceeded to take his place in the box. As one of the leading actors in the tragedy, his revelations were eagerly anticipated. The crowd within the courtroom consisted of mostly fashionably dressed women and girls hardly more than children who were desirous of the recitation concerning the seamy and adulterous relationship.

Tension within the courtroom was raised to a fever pitch as all in attendance listened to his story which was told in a manner plainly and without any pretext to disguise or soften its meaning. John Dunning began quite innocently speaking of his marriage to Mary Elizabeth, who was the daughter of Mr. John Pennington in Dover, Delaware. He advised that their daughter, little Mary Elizabeth, had been born, to them, December 15 of the same year.

Mr. Dunning testified that he was employed by the Associated Press. He and Mary Elizabeth had returned west to San Francisco soon after the wedding so he could assume his new position as manager of the office. It appears from his remarks the marriage had been marred by separations as Mary, on more than one occasion, vacationed in Dover, Delaware. These may have been imposed by Mary Elizabeth as she had a great difficulty with the cosmopolitan environment of San Francisco. It appears that she felt more comfortable in the atmosphere of her hometown. Whatever the reason, it made for openness in a marriage, which in the Victorian Age, was well suited for a "bon vivant" of John Dunning's disposition.

John Dunning's substantive testimony was really rather brief. During his liaison with Cordelia Botkin, which he freely admitted, he shared a domicile at 927 Geary Street. During one of their many conversations he had told Cordelia of some of his wife's characteristics and peculiarities.

Mr. Dunning stated, matter of factly, that:

> my wife is extremely religious and that she was born in an entirely different atmosphere from that in San Francisco . . . she did not understand it and couldn't appreciate it, and that she had a very high idea of morality. . . . (Transcript of Appeal, Criminal No., 632, February 1900, page 638-639).

He espoused to Cordelia about his wife's physical tastes and that there was one she had in particular. Mary Elizabeth it seemed had one passion in life which she could not curtail and it was candy.

Leaving this vein the questioning next turned to his wife's death and from whence he had received the news. He testified that after tearful good-byes between him and Cordelia, he had left San Francisco as a correspondent assigned to the war with Spain in Cuba. Covering the war brought a sense of relief from him for it removed his person from Cordelia's presence. He and Mary Elizabeth had met for a brief time in New York prior to his departure, and after a reconciliation, Mr. Dunning had determined that he would make a clean break with Cordelia and start life anew. He vacillated under scrutiny as to whether he had cut all ties with the West and Cordelia. In fact he admitted there had been correspondence with her during his tenure in Cuba. If nothing else could be said about John Dunning, it would appear that he was a faithless wonder.

On the 13 of August, however, his life would change. He received a cablegram at Ponce, Puerto Rico, informing him of the death of his wife. Little else was said concerning the circumstances, and it was five days hence that he learned the full particulars after arriving in New York.

Two days later, John Dunning arrived in Dover, Delaware, on a train and met with his father-in-law, Attorney-General White, and Detective Bernard McVey. He was at this time shown two anonymous letters and another paper, presumably the wrapper. Perusing each, he became painfully aware of one fact to all certainty: The handwriting on each piece of paper was known to him. All the documents were written by a hand of which he was thoroughly familiar. Cordelia Botkin had written them all, and to this he was certain.

Having bared his soul to the world telling all of his unbridled passions and his shocking immorality, he placed the blame for his wife and her sister's death on the female philanderer. The woman who had once stated:

> I have lived a gay life, with no thought but for pleasure. What others conceived as wrong was no sin to me. For pleasures sake I would stop at nothing, not even divorce court, but I would not stoop to murder (*San Francisco Call,* December 20, 1898).

Obviously in John P. Dunning's eyes she would.

With the substantive examination concluded by the prosecution, the effect on the defense was damning, and its effect rippled through the courtroom as all sensed its impact. The paramour, the rake, and the immoral and amoral beast had spoken. The defense, led by George Knight, girded itself and began the uphill battle necessary to impeach this self-confessed womanizer.

Innocuously, Mr. Knight posed a few superfluous questions regarding the handwriting on the anonymous letters. Mr. Dunning reiterated that it was his firm belief they were written by the defendant Cordelia Botkin. He was questioned as to why he had told Cordelia and his wife they were written by a Mrs. Callumberty. Dunning remarked that this Mrs. C. had made remarks about him shortly after his wife's last departure. The remarks were disparaging in nature, and wanting to conceal his illicit adventures from his wife, he sought subterfuge as a defense. The door was now open, and Knight unrelentingly pressed the moment. Could not Mrs. Seeley have been the author, for it was known she had an intense dislike for Mrs. Botkin because of the relationship between Seeley and Beverly Botkin?

Perhaps there were other women who could have been the author. John Dunning, with naive stupidity, admitted that he has enjoyed the society of a number of women in San Francisco during his tenure here. Seizing the moment, George Knight demanded to know the names of the others Dunning had shared intimate relations. Blatantly Dunning stated that he would have to do some calculating prior to answering Knight's question.

Belatedly it dawned on John Dunning, a lawyer himself, the intent and direction the defense attorney was headed. He began to squirm in his chair. Here was the self-acknowledged philanderer, the user of women trapped and cornered by his own words. If he answered the question, he would show the world that he was a vile scoundrel by violating one of the basic tenets of social intercourse.

Realizing he had his man, George Knight pressed for an answer. The crowded gallery was in hushed silence. All heads pressed forward to hear the spoken words. To his credit, John Dunning did the unexpected: He refused to answer the question. Warned by Judge Cook that refusal meant contempt of court, John Dunning vacillated, unsure of which way to proceed.

In the end, he steadfastly refused to answer George Knight's question, and Judge Cook was left with no recourse. George Knight, for his part, refused to withdraw the question, and a stalemate existed. The attorney had Dunning on the hook and was unrelenting. For the next two days, Dunning was brought to court and asked the same question. Each time he refused and was returned to the county Jail.

Though John Dunning's testimony had been suspended by the course of the action he had chosen, the trial went forward. Testimony on the following day included a number of witnesses called to the witness box to gather the odds and ends in the prosecution's long and complicated circumstantial trial. Mrs. Louise Seeley, Beverly Botkin's alleged lover, took the stand first. She was questioned as to her relationship with the lad. George Knight pressed her concerning events which had taken place during the period of the Dunning (Botkin) affair. She was privy to incidental facts but offered no stunning revelations. Louise also denied steadfastly that she was author of any of the anonymous missives.

Chapter Thirteen

Dunning Sent Back to County Jail: Again Refuses to Answer That Question

Three Delaware witnesses were recalled to the witness stand for the purpose of clarifying earlier testimony. Professor Wolfe was recalled to state that there was no difference between amorphous and crystalline arsenic. Harry Pennington was recalled by the court for the purpose of answering a question which had been forbade in earlier testimony. The court, finding itself in error, recanted and would allow the defense to elicit an answer. Harry was excused when George Knight refused to reintroduce the question. The Honorable John Pennington was recalled to the witness box to verify certain pertinent facts regarding the anonymous letters. With the housecleaning concluded, John Hosmer directed the prosecution on a course to the last phase of its case.

The greater part of December 20 and much of the 21 was devoted to the introduction of the evidence from the handwriting experts. First to be called to the witness box was Mr. Daniel Ames, a handwriting examiner from New York. Described as a venerable writing expert of a thousand trials, he explained how through analysis of unknown and known handwriting samples he had arrived at his conclusions regarding the written evidence in the case.

Daniel Ames painstakingly subjected the gallery to a description of the note in the candy box. Painstakingly, by word and picture, he dissected the "With love to yourself and baby; Mrs. C." note. He described how he would select a single letter and by his usual formula sift through known writing samples.

Placing his work before the jurymen, he attempted to educate them to his process. As the gallery slowly cleared, hoping to escape the heat and boredom of his examination, the jury was held captive. Despite an adverse reaction by Mr. Knight who hated experts, Daniel Ames persevered. His final conclusion was that the defendant, Cordelia Botkin, and no one else had penned the mysterious note.

Carl Eisenschimmel, a second handwriting expert, followed Daniel Ames to the witness stand. Miraculously, the jury was spared this day from his description of muscle recoil and muscular coordination and the other matters which only experts m this line of work share an intimacy. The time for adjournment had arrived and court recessed for the day.

As court reconvened the following day there was no sense of the varied interest which this day would bring. Perched in the witness box was Carl Eisenschimmel ready to resume his exposition regarding the peculiarities of Cordelia Botkin's handwriting. This day George Knight was feeling somewhat under the weather; however, as good attorneys will, he made a valiant effort to keep pace with the witness.

Mr. Eisenschimmel broke Cordelia's handwriting into single letters, combinations of letters, and then into full words. Exhibits flooded the courtroom as he formulated and, then with due consideration to all present, pontificated his final belief. Beyond all reasonable doubt in his mind, Cordelia Botkin, the defendant, was the initiator of all the unknown specimens.

This concluded the morning session and Knight and his colleagues retired to their chambers ragged and worn by this new barrage fired from the prosecution's arsenal of circumstantial evidence. Snarling at the pretense that handwriting evidence had any bearing on this case, but realizing that its impact may have had a profound significance, the defense regrouped and plotted its next course of action.

As the afternoon session of court commenced, the man who the defense had so relentlessly two days previous pursued was recalled to the witness stand. John P. Dunning took his seat and the question regarding his relationships and the names associated with him was once again requested by Judge Cook. By this point, it had become a battle of the strongest will between John Dunning and George

Knight. Who would prevail was the question utmost in the minds of those gathered in the courtroom.

Having pushed the envelope to the limit, George Knight stunned the crowded courtroom. With little ado, he told the Court that he was withdrawing his demand for the names of the women that John Dunning had admittedly shared his intimacy. Murmurs spread through the crowd which had gathered with eager interest. Why after pounding home the point for two days would George Knight acquiesce?

There was no explanation as to why the question had been withdrawn. A supposition could be drawn from this however, and the answer was quite simple. As the days passed George Knight may have realized that this man who was a self-confessed philanderer by his mere refusals was being elevated to martyrdom. The real thrust, on the other hand, may have lain in the fact that George Knight was suffering from illness. Shortly after this, he withdrew for the day and the completion of the cross-examination was undertaken by his co-counsel, Frank McGowan.

Mr. McGowan was definitely not of the same stature or class as George Knight. Where Knight was demonstrative in his questioning, McGowan was denigrating. His disgusting courtroom antics by any standard elevated John P. Dunning from a miserable wretch to a point of decency. Grasping at straws, McGowan pushed the question of John Dunning and Cordelia Botkin's intimacy to a point of indecency. On more than one occasion McGowan brought forward facts which were clearly beyond the scope of any rational questioning by a defense attorney. Reprimanded several times by Judge Cook, McGowan plodded forward with a harshness that stunned even the hardest spectator.

By his own incompetence, Frank McGowan, with all indifference and ineptitude, elicited the most damaging testimony which John Dunning had presented thus far. Only a first-year law student under severe stress and suffering from mental turpitude would have desired to know, in fact demanded, "Why was John Dunning so hostile toward Mrs. Botkin?"

Stunned, the gallery, the prosecutor, the Judge, and the defendant awaited his answer. John Dunning mustering all the poise that a man in his predicament could effectuate answered in a clear, concise tone.

> I came here with no thought of vengeance on the woman. I came here with no hatred toward her, but with a sense of duty that I owed the dead and a purpose to compensate as far as I may for offenses in the past (*The Call*, December 22, 1898).

Continuing in this vein the witness remarked extemporaneously that he was convinced by all that he had seen that Cordelia was implicated in his wife's death. John Dunning "begged that McGowan believe that it was his duty, not pleasure, that impelled him to become an accuser of Mrs. Botkin" (*The Call*, December 22, 1898).

In disbelief the gallery was further treated to another example of Frank McGowan's stupidity. He was not satisfied with the boomerang which had just hit him full in the face, or he had not realized its full impact.

Without hesitation Mr. McGowan asked John Dunning if he could answer when he first had a suspicion toward Mrs. Botkin as the poisoner. Dunning in all sincerity replied. "He knew Cordelia had committed the crimes within one hour after he reached Dover and was, then and there, convinced of her guilt" (*The Call*, December 22, 1898).

Mr. McGowan was able to ascertain one positive element in his berating and belittling of Dunning. The fact that John Dunning and Cordelia did act in joint collusion to mislead Dunning's wife. Letters which John Dunning had sent Cordelia following his departure from San Francisco and those while in Puerto Rico were admitted into evidence for whatever purpose they might serve. Dunning was then released from the witness stand, and his contempt of court was set aside by Judge Cook.

One can only imagine what George Knight's reaction may have been to his colleagues self-destruction of Cordelia Botkin's case as any personal conversations between the two were not for public record. Slim at best, the chances for an acquittal or total dismissal of the charges were severely damaged by an inept co-counsel. Mercifully for Cordelia Botkin, Frank McGowan demurred from further cross-examination of the final witness for the day.

Theodore Kytka, a pen artist and photographer, was the last prosecution witness. Shown various known samples and unknown exemplars Kytka with the customary, painful explanations of a handwriting expert identified the fact that through comparison he had determined they were made by one person. Asked if he had identified the person, he testified all the writing were those of the defendant, Cordelia Botkin.

Cross-examined by C. M. Wheeler, the junior most member of the defense team, Kytka stood fast and the questioning was profitless. All that one can say about C. M. Wheeler is that he gave a clever imitation of George Knight in stance. His questioning was inane but at least it was palatable, unlike Frank McGowan.

With the conclusion of Mr. Wheeler's cross-examination, Mr. Hosmer rose and stated simply, "If your Honor please, the prosecution rests its case." Caught unawares, which was no surprise, Frank McGowan stated that the defense was unready to proceed. Judge Cook with great wisdom, allowed that as the day was late, court would be in recess. The defense was expected to begin promptly the next day, December 22.

As the court attendees filed from the courthouse one could sense from the general conversation that the prosecution had woven a case strong enough to warrant a conviction. Few had seen circumstantial cases which were stronger. The links in the chain of events had been fabricated so precisely by the prosecution and the collateral evidence presented in such a way that it was connected beyond a reasonable doubt.

Through the trials and tribulations of John Dunning during the past three days, Cordelia Botkin had been surprisingly stoic and withdrawn. Cordelia Botkin was not of the cloth that would let statements concerning her go unchallenged. In the past she had been quite vociferous in her condemnation of those who dared to assail her person.

True to form, Cordelia could not hold her countenance until she reached the witness box. Possibly she had been warned by her counsel to maintain a quiet and unemotional posture. Unfortunately, Cordelia was not a person to be pigeonholed for any period of time.

Cordelia had held within her days of frustration. Though she had a basic dislike and distrust of newspapers and their people, she spewed forth her account of the friendship she had had with John P. Dunning. It was, as usual from Cordelia, slanted and filled with chilling prospective revelations of how she viewed life.

She stated that:

> I was a friend to him during the dark days. . . . There was nothing wrong in my friendship for Mr. Dunning. It

was open, free from complications and there should be no suspicion of immorality attached to it. . . . The little I did for Mr. Dunning was prompted by pity and by a kindly feeling for him in his misfortune. . . . But I now fear that I over estimated his manhood. . . . His conduct while on the witness stand convinced me that I attributed to him more of the qualities of gentlemen than he seems to possess. . . .

His ingratitude I should have passed over, but his aspersion against my character cannot go by unnoticed and without a word of protest. . . . He well knows that I expressed the desire that he rejoin his wife and fulfill his duty to her and to his child. . . .

I found no special interest in the testimony of the experts. . . . The prosecution did not introduce as an exemplar of my writing the words 'John P. Dunning'. . . . I wonder why? . . . I shall prove conclusively that I am not the author of either of the letters. When I am called to the witness stand. I shall be able to establish my innocence" (*San Francisco Examiners*, December 22, 1898).

Chapter Fourteen

Mrs. Cordelia Botkin Pleads With Her Judges for Her Life

Cordelia Botkin's ramblings to the press set the stage for the following morning. Whereas the prosecution in its attempts to prove her guilt had presented sixty-eight witnesses, the defense called but sixteen. Waiving its right to an opening statement, the defense entered upon its quest immediately. The gallery in hushed tones awaited the multitude of witnesses which would place Cordelia elsewhere at the time of the crime. This had been promised by the defense prior to the opening of the trial and was eagerly anticipated.

The plethora of alibi witnesses would never materialize. Instead the assembled gallery would be treated to mostly inconsequential and inane testimony from a variety of minor characters. As court convened, the first witness of the day was called, Dr. George F. Tyrrell. Dr. Tyrrell testified that he had attended to a sickly Cordelia Botkin on July 31, between three and five o'clock. His recollection was that he had responded to the Victoria Hotel having been summoned by the telephone; the caller was none other than Cordelia Botkin.

The good doctor told of the symptoms expressed by Cordelia Botkin, her manner, her dress, et cetera. He had in recollection ministered to her in a short period of time and spent the majority of an hour in idle conversation. With the inconsequential facts, elucidated, as a physician, he was asked "was he aware of the symptoms of arsenic poisoning?" Responding in the affirmative, Dr. Tyrrell was then asked what procedure, if any, would be necessary to prove death by arsenic poisoning. He affirmed that there was but one procedure, which would be conclusive, and that would be an autopsy.

Having concluded his examination, George Knight gave way to the prosecutor, John Hosmer. Dr. Tyrrell was pressed for the date of his visit and the intimation was that the date might have been other than July 31. He attempted to maintain his positive manner, but Mr. Hosmer asked about Tyrrell's appointment book which would prove beyond a shadow of doubt the date. Dr. Tyrrell produced the book, but no entry existed concerning the alleged patient, Cordelia Botkin. His reasoning when pressed for not noting this visit was that he did not expect to be paid, which was rather odd.

Pressed further by the prosecutor, he was asked if he recalled a conversation with a Seattle reporter while on vacation later that summer. George Tyrrell refused to acknowledge that he had told the reporter "Mrs. Botkin could have gone out, that she was not too ill for that" (*San Francisco Call*, December 23, 1898). The questioning turned next to the doctor's posture regarding arsenical poisoning. It was determined that he had never treated an arsenic case, and therefore he was no expert. Severely chastised by the prosecutor for attempting to portray himself as such, he did maintain his stance as to the only sure way of determining an arsenical death, an autopsy. Dr. Tyrrell was released from further inquiry as his testimony was determined to be inconsequential to the facts thus far presented.

The superintendent of the San Francisco mail service, Thomas W. Ford, was the next witness for the defense. Mr. Ford was truly remarkable for his attempts to convince the jurors that the mysterious package had not passed through the U.S. Mail. He maintained that, though the package had what appeared to be a San Francisco postmark, he was not sure that it had come through the city. Thomas Ford was the epitome of bureaucracy for the age.

He recited in detail how packages are received and the number of hands through which they pass. Unless packaged properly, he contended that a box of soft candy would not survive a transcontinental journey. His testimony was bombastic and no doubt left the common man with a total lack of trust for the postal service. A package with the postmark SAN FRAN–-had traversed three thousand miles of travel, and Ford was telling all it was a figment of their imagination.

Following Thomas Ford to the witness box was John P. Dunning and Mrs. Grace Harris. Mr. Dunning was recalled by Mr. Hosmer to refute Mr. Ford's testimony. His testimony was short, simple and to the point. He had told Cordelia Botkin on a number of occasions that Mrs. Dunning and the child had left San Francisco and were residing and would remain in Dover, Delaware. The purpose of his testimony was thus: It showed that Cordelia, living in San Francisco, was aware of the addressee in Dover, Delaware, and could have sent the package.

George Knight's purpose for calling Mrs. Harris to the witness box was to attack her credibility. Knight was still blistering from her former testimony in their previous encounter. His attacks on Grace Harris had little to do with her direct testimony. Knight's sole purpose was an attempt to embarrass her by innuendo. Judge Cook in a chivalrous manner denied Knight his quest and she was released.

Cordelia Botkin's brother-in-law, W. H. Robards was next to occupy the witness box. He offered a positive note to the defense case by testifying that Cordelia could not have posted the anonymous letter of June 1897. At that time she was visiting his family in Eureka, California, and with exception of one day, had not left the residence for one month. On its face this was prima facia evidence in Cordelia's favor. Unfortunately, it would be for naught as there was a mailbag suspended from the gangplank of all steamers traveling up and down the California coast. All mail deposited in these bags received a San Francisco postmark once they reached that city. Cordelia had traveled to and from Eureka on a steamer, thus negating this point.

Two physicians, Dr. W. F. McNatt and Dr. William B. Deas, next occupied the witness box. Both were experts in the field of arsenic poisoning and both bolstered in succession the defense contention that the only sure way to determine death by arsenic poisoning was by autopsy. The defense it appeared was fixated on this fact, and nothing would alter its course.

Several other minor players would occupy the witness box throughout the day. The defense it would appear was attempting to tidy the house and put contentions and suppositions to rest regarding Cordelia Botkin's opportunity to commit the crime. Following the good doctors in quick succession James Walkington, a floor walker at the City of Paris, Professor Theodore Wolfe, the Delaware chemist, and Chief I. W. Lees, and finally Mrs. Harris would pass through the inquisition box and then be released.

The day was growing late and having listened to a number of dull, unenergetic witnesses, the gallery had begun to weary. Heads nodded and all present in the tightly packed courtroom fought to remain awake. With no foreshadowing of events to come, George Knight rose from his chair. With only the briefest of pause he called out the name "Mrs. Cordelia Botkin."

Caught by surprise, heads snapped to attention as if pulled by invisible strings. There was rustling of silk and satin as both men and women alike leaned forward in their seats with eager anticipation. This was the long awaited moment, the moment when Cordelia Botkin would take center stage. Spectators within the courtroom patted themselves on the back for their perseverance. Finally the woman charged with deaths of the Dover women would tell her own story. It was for many the moment of truth.

All eyes focused on Cordelia as she moved across the court to the witness box. For the first time the gathered throng viewed the alleged murderess unveiled. She had a pair of flashing black eyes that betrayed little of her nature. At first glance one would say that from stature, countenance, and demeanor she was for her forty-odd years remarkable. In no way, shape, or form would anyone speak of her as tender or loveable, however.

It was readily apparent from the outset after taking the oath that the jury was viewing a formidable woman. She was without question a consummate actress well suited for the role she was about to play. Having completed the oath administered by the clerk, Cordelia Botkin drew her chair sideways to bring it closer to the jury. Having fully gained their attention, she struck a pose, very similar to the first days of the trial. Cordelia wished all who viewed her to perceive her as the downtrodden and persecuted innocent hounded by a vengeful prosecution.

Her testimony as it commenced was indeed well rehearsed. It was evident to all that her facts were well committed to memory and had been for some time. At times from her ability to let the words flow so quickly, it appeared to those in attendance that she was reading a written statement. Her testimony began with George Knight asking the usual interrogatory questions to ascertain background information. Then with few additional prompts, Cordelia was given free reign to tell her tale. Speaking in measured tones, Cordelia's voice at times was deep, harsh, and with a hint of anxious masculinity. Her manner justified the sobriquet of the "little English woman," for though she had never been further east than

Missouri, she had succeeded in affecting that speech pattern by which Americans perceive the English.

She began her story with a description of that day three years past in Golden Gate Park. Cordelia recounted the chance meeting which engendered the ongoing relationship with John P. Dunning and how after words and cordialities were exchanged, the two had parted company. There was no vision of a blossoming friendship, as she termed it.

When next they met, Cordelia was living at 2217 Bush Street. It was a chance meeting on the street as she neared her residence. A man who at first she did not recognize tipped his hat and bade her greetings. It was sometime before she realized who he was. The two spoke and walked together a brief time and then once again parted company. From this encounter, a friendship had ensued, but to Cordelia there was no sense of a burgeoning relationship. Over the course of the next three years, the friendship would escalate as she sought to help this poor lost soul who had fallen on hard times. She assisted him financially from time to time and attempted to instill within him the self-confidence to survive.

According to Cordelia, Dunning had used money belonging to the Associated Press to feed his needs and was in fear of the law. There was nothing between the two acquaintances except the pity one soul may feel for another during times of adversity. She was quick to add though Dunning was a constant companion during this time, her son, Beverly, was always present, and therefore any alleged amorous trysts were not real but imagined.

She rambled for a considerable time and detailed her movements of residences during this initial period. Beginning at 2217 Bush Street, she told of her brief hiatus with her sister in Oakland while John Dunning was employed in Salt Lake City, and of her short residency at 1001 Bush Street upon her return to the city. Cordelia spoke of 927 Geary Street and of the alleged activities which occurred within its walls. She denied any orgies or distasteful behavior, which was in her eyes beneath the dignity of a lady.

In June 1897, Cordelia had traveled to Humboldt County to stay with another sister while she (Cordelia) recovered from the effects of a mild illness. Accompanied by Almira Ruoff, to whom she referred as her personal nurse, Cordelia remained there for one month. Cordelia became convinced during this convalescence that she was suffering from pneumonia and requested a physician. A local doctor, Thomas Stone, was summoned and administered to

Cordelia's needs. Subsequent to this examination in which he prescribed calomel and morphine, there had been a brief discussion concerning poison.

Cordelia questioned the physician specifically about morphine, which she noted was a poisonous substance. Dr. Stone advised that as a medicinal given under the proper guidance, there would be no adverse effects. She denied any conversation regarding any other types of poisons or poisonous compounds even in jest. Any testimony regarding any such alleged conversation was pure fabrication.

Mrs. Botkin professed she noted a significant change in her health by the end of the month, and believing she had recovered sufficiently, she returned to San Francisco. On her return she resided briefly at the Ralston Home, 1222 Pine Street. Remaining there but a short time, Cordelia related that she next moved to 1224 Hyde Street, staying at this residence the remainder of 1897. In April of 1898 Cordelia had procured her final residence in the city at the Victoria Hotel, Hyde Street and California Street.

Cordelia Botkin's preparation was meticulous and her recitation given with such rapidity that the court stenographers were strained to the fullest to record all her words. Stopping to take a breath, Cordelia queried George Knight, "Is all this stupid, or shall I go on." Closing one's eyes and listening to Cordelia banter, one would have no indication that her narration was not being given at a church social. Assured by George Knight that her actions were not stupid, she turned next to the crux of the case against her. Referring to the alleged purchase of the candy at the George Haas Candy Store, she espoused total flat denial. Quite succinctly, her answer was "I never did, I was never in the shop in all my life" (*San Francisco Examiner*, December 23, 1898).

With this said, she next contradicted Miss Lizzie Livernash. Cordelia had concealed nothing from the reporter. When told by Miss Livernash that she was suspected of the death of Mrs. John P. Dunning Cordelia admitted that she had become hysterical. Naturally shocked by this blasphemous news, she admitted that she had become unconscious. Cordelia denied flatly however that any conversations regarding her involvement in the deaths had occurred between her and Lizzie Livernash. She considered Miss Livernash a friend and confidant and was very perplexed by Livernash's journalistic sabotage.

Cordelia was questioned regarding the purported purchase of the infamous handkerchief which had accompanied the death dealing chocolates. With extreme candor, she denied the purchase of this item from the City of Paris. She then intimated that she had never had any package delivered to her from this store while in residence at the Victoria Hotel.

As if following a script, Cordelia's attention now turned to the quarrels with Louise Seeley. She stated that Louise was infatuated with her son, Beverly. Fourteen years his senior, this poor naive lad was no match for a brazen hussy of Seeley's ilk. All went well at first and there was no animosity between the two until Cordelia suggested that Louise Seeley find a paramour more her age. Mrs. Seeley vehemently objected to the suggestion. Harsh words were exchanged and from that moment on, Louise Seeley became her bitter enemy. Cordelia felt that Mrs. Seeley would stoop at nothing short of implicating her in murder to satisfy her vengeful heart.

The day ended on this dramatic note. Cordelia had confronted her accusers, and though she showed moments of vulnerability and flashes of extreme temper, for the most part she had exhibited the demeanor of a persecuted woman. Cordelia did her best to portray herself as the innocent victim in the whole sordid affair. The hour was late and court was adjourned for the day. Smiling and self-composed Cordelia Botkin would re-ascend the witness stand on Friday, December 23, 1898. The largest crowd to date assembled within and without the courtroom for a chance to hear her amazing tales. Having refuted the prosecution's witnesses on this first day in the witness box, she was prepared to continue her case.

As court convened for the day, Cordelia would be forced to wait in the wings. The first witness of the day was Captain Callunder of the Morse's Detective Agency. His testimony had little to do with the guilt or innocence of Cordelia but rather was centered on Mrs. Grace Harris. George Knight, for all his stature as a prominent defense counsel, was totally fixated upon this woman who had bested him. Rather than attempting to impeach her testimony, Knight elicited the fact that Mrs. Harris had been the center of a controversy at her previous employer. In fact under suspicion for improper activities, Grace Harris had been terminated. By supposition, George Knight made every attempt he could muster to impugn Grace Harris's character.

Rather than trying the case on its merit, George Knight with insolence attacked a second prosecution witness. The second witness of the day to assume his position in the witness box was J. W. Bird, a general merchant in the city. A brother-in-law of Kittie

Dettner, he was called to say mean things and not for any substantive testimony (*The Call,* December 24, 1898). Under purposeful examination by George Knight, Mr. Bird intimated the fact that Kittie Dettner was known to tell falsehoods. To Bird her reputation for dishonesty was "legions." She was to his mind a scandalous person who would stoop to any degree to present false information. J. W. Bird was, unfortunately for Mr. Knight, impeached by the prosecution during its cross-examination. Mr. Bird informed the court that not only was Mrs. Dettner's behavior scandalous but so was that of her mother and her grandmother. The import of his testimony was somewhat negated by his final outburst.

With this concluded, Cordelia was recalled to the witness stand and rapt attention was directed towards her as she began the final session of her examination by George Knight. Briefly summarized, her testimony centered on John P. Dunning and his time in Salt Lake City. Letters had been exchanged between the two, and it was during this period that the first anonymous letter received by Mary Elizabeth had been transmitted to Cordelia for her insight. Having scrutinized the letter, she now denied as emphatically as she had all the other suppositions that she was the author of any anonymous letters. Questioned directly on another point by George Knight, Cordelia succinctly denied any association with the infamous chocolates or the mysterious package which was mailed to Dover, Delaware.

Switching his tact, George Knight moved forward to questioning in regards to arsenic. Having previously admitted in newspaper interviews that she had purchased arsenic for the purpose of bleaching a hat, Cordelia Botkin now embarked upon a new course. With no hesitation, she boldly denied purchasing arsenic on the first of June 1898. In addition to this and without the slightest reservation, she denied ever being in the Owl Drug Store. Identification of her as the person who entered the Owl Drugs notwithstanding, Cordelia denied being the purchaser of arsenic on the date in question. Further she denied knowing Frank Grey, or for that matter, ever having been in his presence with or without John P. Dunning.

The drug register told all, but Cordelia with downcast eyes, the humbled miscreant, staunchly denied that "Mrs. Botkin, Victoria Hotel, Hyde and California St. 2 ounces arsenic 073198" was she. Her stupidity on the matter defies imagination. The jury, for its part, must have looked upon her in disbelief. A druggist of unimpuned character had faced her eye to eye and identified her as the purchaser of the arsenic.

Her testimony was perplexing. She denied all that the prosecution witnesses presented. Some bit of acquiescence would no doubt have gone in her favor. Perhaps, some of the witnesses had been misinformed or, by chance, coerced by Chief Lees and his gendarmes, but not all of them.

Birdie Price was the stellar example of the classic denial. Having done nothing to harm Cordelia, she was portrayed as a person of less than moral stature. Mrs. Price had seen Cordelia coming from the street into the *Victoria,* but she was made to appear inept and incompetent. Cordelia meant to cover all loose ends and for her this meant all. She reiterated, "I was sick, I pulled myself together . . . bought bread fruit and some drugs at the chemist shop . . . I met Mrs. Price on the stairs. She remonstrated me for not taking care of myself. . . ." Cordelia's watchword was *denial* and she stuck to it (*San Francisco Examiner*, December 24, 1898).

Her final course was to assail John P. Dunning personally. With little remorse, she flailed her former paramour as a remorseless womanizer, gambler, and drinker. Asked if she had written any letters addressed John P. Dunning, Cordelia stated any correspondence with him was always addressed J. P. Dunning, Esq.

She stated she too had received anonymous letters much like her counterpart Mary Elizabeth Dunning. Cordelia had an answer for each and every question asked. She readily admitted that she had asked Almira Ruoff about postage for packages. This was for a package however that she wished to mail to Humboldt County, not Dover, Delaware. Cordelia had a response in the positive sense for anything which appeared detrimental for her defense and might cast a negative connotation.

In conclusion, she advised that there never was talk of a marriage between her and Mr. Dunning. Divorce to Cordelia, the devoted spouse, was out of the question. George Knight asked what advice, if any, had Cordelia given to Mr. Dunning regarding his marriage. The response was typical Cordelia Botkin. Speaking in motherly tones she had told John Dunning to go back to his wife, stop drinking, and do the best for himself and them. She knew even then that Mrs. Dunning was too good for him. Cordelia Botkin had painted a portrait of herself as a saint, a Christian of the highest moral fiber.

Having thrown down the gauntlet with her total denial of all facets of the prosecution's case, Cordelia had set the stage for impeachment. As Mr. Hosmer rose from his chair, all present sat in eager anticipation of a lengthy, grueling and time consuming examination. By her plausible deniability, Cordelia had hurt her own case. Refuting all, even those points which had been proven such as the testimony by Frank Grey who knew her by face and name, she had, no doubt, left questions in the mind of the jury.

Her cross-examination was far from what was expected. Driving at the details of her association with John Dunning and showing that there had been much more than an innocent liaison between the two star-crossed lovers, John A. Hosmer exhibited gallantry. This was the Victorian Age and Mr. Hosmer, unlike his counterpart George Knight, showed the perfect male conduct of the time.

Proving his points concerning the inconsistency in Cordelia's testimony and concerning the many witnesses who had testified, he withdrew from the asking of annoying and impertinent questions. Minor admissions were ascertained from Cordelia Botkin during the course of his cross-examination. Grudgingly she was forced to concede that she had frequented the City of Paris and had purchased items on occasion. Having disputed much of the testimony given by Dunning, Lizzie Livernash, and Almira Ruoff in her direct examination, Cordelia acknowledged that much of what they had said did have substance although she did diametrically oppose Dunning's testimony concerning the fact of ever being told that Mrs. Dunning had a love of chocolate. With this concluded, John Hosmer stunned the waiting crowd and for that matter even Judge Cook. Evidently, the judge had thought that Cordelia's cross-examination would be quite extensive and severe, and in anticipation of this he had set aside the entire day.

Therefore all in attendance were surprised when after laying the basis for impeachment and contradiction Prosecutor Hosmer stated simply, "That's all." There was a stunned silence within the courtroom. The gallery, and even George Knight, was stunned by the sudden closure. As Cordelia Botkin was released from further testimony, George Knight addressed the court and stated the defense case was completed.

As court recessed until the following Tuesday, due to the Christmas holiday, Chief I. W. Lees put the reasoning for the prosecution's short endeavor in perspective. Simply stated:

> The lawyers debated a long time whether to ask a single question. There was no use in trying to break her down, for she is an intelligent woman and has had all these months to think over her role. A person would become letter perfect in the dictionary in less time than that. . . . There was nothing to be gained by badgering her (*San Francisco Examiner,* December 24, 1898).

Feeling she had eluded Mr. Hosmer and those aligned against her, Cordelia once again felt it necessary to speak in her own defense. With a ready smile, a genial mannerism, and cheery words she related facts pertaining to her latest ordeal.

> Going into the witness box and being asked what one has done and questioned about what one has not done is an experience no woman with ordinary common sense is supposed to do in court. Yet I was glad yesterday and today of the opportunity of being placed under oath. . . . To a woman who has had no desire to violate the code of morality, to a woman of refinement, and self-respect; the sting in any reflection on her character is beyond the power of any human being to describe...God alone knows what sorrow unjust accusations have caused me...(S*an Francisco Examiner,* December 24, 1898).

Chapter Fifteen

Botkin Is Guilty of the Cruel Delaware Murders

As the final sessions of the court loomed near, Cordelia Botkin with all the pomp and circumstance of a queen made her grand entrance. Elated by her performance of the previous two days, she was filled with smiles, chattiness, and a renewed vigor. The first order of business was the prosecution's rebuttal and a ragtag group of unimposing witnesses was to adorn the witness box this day.

Both sides would have some success as the prosecution would attempt to undermine the defense's contentions concerning the fateful day of July 31. The defense would then counter the prosecution's assertion that Cordelia was the author of the anonymous letters. It would prove all too interesting in a very unassuming way. George Knight was veritably incorrigible in his attacks on the rights of the prosecution witnesses as they passed through the witness box.

This day he was left to his bantering and questionable rages at the prosecution witnesses. Judge Cook had once been quoted in reference to Knight that the "only way to control him was with a club." On this day there was little effort to curb the flamboyant attorney as he rode roughshod on the witnesses and opposing attorneys. His manner once again however would prove his undoing and once again the defense would self-destruct.

John Hosmer began the morning in an effort to impeach the testimony of Dr. Tyrrell. The first witness called was Miss Maggie Smith, a cook at the Victoria Hotel. She was to impeach Tyrrell regarding his testimony concerning the date of his visit to Cordelia. Described as a meager, mincing woman, wearing spectacles, she was asked if she could identify the good doctor. After scrutinizing him in a most slow and deliberate manner, Miss Smith stated that he was the physician who had attended to Mrs. Botkin on Monday or Tuesday, not Sunday. Her reasoning for the affirmative response was that Mrs. Birdie Price never left her in charge on Sunday. She was on the day of the doctor's visit in charge. With this confirmation, the prosecution quietly turned Miss Smith over to George Knight.

Filled with himself this day and believing that he was invincible, George Knight prepared to pounce upon this mouse of a woman. As in times past as the old adage goes, the early bird was about to catch the worm. Instead of leaving well enough alone, George Knight began poking into areas better left alone. Through his thorough questioning of Maggie Smith, it was elicited that Mrs. Botkin claiming illness had taken dinner in her room on Sunday, July 31. This occurred after five o'clock, well outside the time of the candy purchase.

Not satisfied to this point, George Knight pressed forward. He raised the presumption that Miss Smith did not know that Cordelia had left her room, because he reasoned that she never saw Cordelia come back in the afternoon. It has been said that ignorance is bliss, but stupidity for a defense attorney is incomprehensible. By his own inane behavior, George Knight was about to receive a blow right between his eyes.

Surprisingly the prosecution was unaware of how Miss Smith would respond. The answer to Knight's impertinence brought elation. Miss Maggie Smith, the unpretentious cook and housemaid, delivered a deathblow to the defense. She stated in a quiet but firm tone that on Sunday, July 31, between three and four o'clock she was standing behind Mrs. Birdie Price. At that time, she witnessed Cordelia Botkin enter the hotel carrying a bundle of packages. She thus confirmed the testimony of Birdie Price who had been persecuted and castigated by George Knight. To reiterate something said before, parrots and lawyers sometimes talk too much.

Knocked from his perch and with feathers ruffled, George Knight endeavored to change his course. He would receive high marks in a different area regarding the anonymous letters. On firmer ground, his questioning of various witnesses established some doubt as to whether Cordelia Botkin could have been the author. Try as he could, John Hosmer could not secure a unanimous foothold relating to this viable evidence. From postal officials, the prosecution did prove that Ferry Station would be the point of origin. Further the prosecution showed through supposition that Mrs. Botkin would have been in the station at the approximate time of the mailing of the "mysterious package." Also established was the fact that candy packaged properly or improperly would with little doubt have survived the transcontinental journey.

There were but a few further incidental witnesses during the rest of the trial's last day. Among them was poor Grace Harris who was George Knight's favorite aversion during the course of the trial. Questioned as to transmission of packages from the store to outside points, she spoke briefly concerning procedures and was finally set free. The most interesting and long awaited witness was Mrs. Clara Arbogast. Cast in the role of the other woman, the gallery perked to hear the slightest indecency or innuendo. Clara was the woman who had been referred to repeatedly as the person who had so charmed Cordelia's husband, Welcome A., that he had shunned the defendant in her time of need and desperation.

Her testimony had little substance concerning the main issue. To Mr. Knight in questioning, she referred to Mr. Botkin's and her relationship as "platonic" not "plutonic." Articulate as he was, George Knight did suffer from some foibles in life. She emphatically denied being responsible in anyway for that matter in any involvement in the death of Mrs. Dunning. As to the anonymous letters she steadfastly refused to admit authorship. Firm and precise, she was a foe that George Knight could not intimidate. Try as he would, she thwarted his advances at every turn. Shown writings of her own depicting the capital "C" the defense claimed there was a remarkable resemblance between this and the anonymous note. One letter does not make a note or a lengthy correspondence, and it was apparent to all, try as he would, George Knight was grasping at straws. As the day passed and the rest of the rebuttal witnesses came and went and as the pace slowed, the gallery thinned.

Prior to the day's close, Attorney Knight brought forth a letter which had been delivered this very day. The letter brought by messenger was addressed to Mrs. Botkin in care of her attorney, George Knight. As with all the other letters in the case it was anonymous.

It intimated in short that Clara Arbogast had received a sum of money from Mrs. Botkin. The letter summarized that a conspiracy existed between Louise Seeley and Clara Arbogast to remove Cordelia Botkin, denoting that a conspiracy therefore existed. True to the last, the *State of California v. Cordelia Botkin* had a strange twist. With the reception of this letter, which was ignored by the court, the case reached its conclusion. Summations would follow the next day as the court went into adjournment.

The last word of the day was left to Cordelia. Though her fate was to be within days if not hours given to twelve just men, Cordelia felt she must lash out at someone. This day the receptors of her vengeance were Mr. Botkin and Mrs. Clara Arbogast.

She began her oration (which is presented only in part):

> How did I feel when I heard the name of that woman called; saw her sweep into the courtroom and for the first time in my life was face to face with her? How can I tell you or make you understand? I underwent a series of conflicting emotions. . . . She robbed me of the love and devotion of my husband and broke up the peace of our once happy home. . . . Mrs. Arbogast is not only the cause of the estrangement between Mr. Botkin and myself, but she is responsible for his desertion of me at this time, when his place is at my side. . . . I do not charge Mrs. Arbogast or anyone else of the crime, but on the motive proposition her interest was certainly strong. The conduct of the woman in court today made me think that if she had anything to do with the crime she felt that she has made a success in placing it at my door (*San Francisco Examiner*, December 28, 1898).

With that said, Cordelia Botkin returned to her dismal quarters at the Branch County Jail to await the commencement of court activities. The next two days, December 28 and 29, would be filled with the rhetoric of the opposing counsels. Taking center stage, these four men learned in the law would reiterate the case which had been so tediously argued over the last two weeks.

Attorney-General Robert C. White of Delaware was the first to speak. His lengthy opening argument occupied fully the first morning of summations. Meticulously, he proceeded step by step to trace the people's case. In a precise painstaking manner, he logically linked the chain of circumstantial evidence. The salient points of each witness, from the cases initiation in Dover, Delaware, to the final moments in San Francisco, were presented to the jury for its consideration.

Though the least articulate of the men who would attempt to sway the jury, Mr. White, performing on foreign soil, did well for someone unfamiliar with the State of California and local attorney flamboyance. Having presented the evidence of guilt, Robert White closed his argument for conviction of Cordelia with the following:

> . . . I say to you if you believe from the evidence that the defendant is guilty of this crime as charged, then it is your duty to render your verdict of guilty as much as it would be render a verdict of not guilty if you believed her innocent . . . for it is written that 'whosoever takes a brothers blood shall suffer death.' The laws of California demand it because it is there written that he who takes a brother's life shall suffer death (*San Francisco Examiner,* December 29, 1898).

This closed the opening phase of the summations. Twelve men tried and true had been chosen and it was now their duty to decide Cordelia Botkin's fate. It had been reported by the press and court-savvy attendees that Mr. White's speech was not up to California's standards, and this may have been true. He was a country boy who spoke in clear, concise tones and relied on fact, not conjecture, to make a point. One, however, within the courtroom was clearly affected. Cordelia Botkin, the accused murderess, was left in tears and was apparently inconsolable as Robert White minutely hammered home point after point.

As the afternoon session convened, Mr. George Knight, the antitheses of his southern counterpart, rose to address the jury and the assembled listeners. Eloquent and forceful, he made much more of an impressive appearance. With a vengeance second to none, George Knight whittled away at the prosecution's seemingly concrete circumstantial case. Knight put numerous witnesses and their invincible testimony to the test during his discourse. He freely quoted from the Bible while attempting to create that doubt so important to swaying the minds of a jury. Rather than trying the case on its own merit, he made many disparaging remarks about the prosecution and its witnesses.

Chief Lees, though on the periphery, was attacked as being incompetent and negligent. Mr. Knight called the performance of the police officials a dereliction of duty and accused them of the suppression of evidence. He alluded to Lees as "the ole subonneted, decayed, senile fossil . . . who blotted a portion of the evidence . . . that might prove the innocence of my client . . . ." (*The Call*, December 29, 1898). George Knight dwelt long and hard on the Delaware chemist, Theodore Wolfe, and his variance with Mr. Price of San Francisco regarding lump and powdered arsenic. He was very secure in his element, at this point using the oratorical venue to attack those who sought to castigate his client. He spared no one on the prosecution side with his virulent and aggressive assault.

In order, he attacked the druggist David Green, John Pennington and his conglomeration of Delaware witnesses, and finally, John Dunning. For this man, George Knight was malicious to the extreme and attacked all aspects of this person. George Knight portrayed John Dunning in such a way that all present must have winced.

Mr. Knight expressed chagrin regarding the fact that

> They attacked Mrs. Botkin's character because of her life with Dunning. This was only permitted in such a case to show motive. What say you of the other nine women who have shared his bed and charms and whose names have not been mentioned (*The Call,* December 29, 1898)?

Dunning was not the only person that Knight subjected to cruel taunts and criticism. Mr. Ames, the handwriting analyst, did not escape unscathed. In paying his respects George Knight portrayed him as thusly:

> If ever a brutal wretch lived on this earth it is that penharlot Dan Ames. There is a man who would have no compunction in swearing away a human life. . . . (*The Call,* December 29, 1898).

George Knight's tuperative abuse of the prosecution was all but concluded at this point. He had but one left to belittle and this was his whipping boy (or girl in this case), Mrs. Grace Harris. This was a woman who had clearly "gotten under George Knight's skin." As he prepared to close his blistering assault, Knight called her "a cat–

a degenerate female with a peculiar mentality like that of the sweet pea girl, whose only desire was to gain notoriety at any cost (*The Call*, December 29, 1898).

Closing his argument, George Knight appealed to the jury for justice, not mercy. He personalized the defense case by citing the case of Dreyfuss in France and of Florence Maybrick in England. Both were examples of innocent persons convicted of crimes in which they had no part. His final note was the sounding board for acquittal:

> . . . Mrs. Botkin was suffering because she had not led that life of high ideals we all admire so much. She was not on trial, however, for her violation of the marriage laws, but for murder. Blot out her previous sins and try her by the evidence (*The Call,* December 29, 1898).

The day was thus concluded and all waited in anticipation of the next morning. As the dying days of 1898 flitted by, the trial was reaching its final moments. Having to this point been relegated in lawyer parlance, to "second chair," Senator Frank McGowan was about to embark upon a bitter tirade. Occupying the floor the entire day, Frank McGowan, who began with a beseeching of justice not mercy for his client, denigrated himself and the defense to a new level. George Knight had been forceful in his attack on the prosecution, but he had not been vengeful. Frank McGowan was no George Knight, and his attack was a volatile tirade which defied imagination.

He portrayed Cordelia Botkin as the chaste martyr who was being assailed by a virulent prosecutor and his gnomes who sought to lay the death of Mary Elizabeth Dunning at her door. Mr. McGowan ignored all that was obvious and attacked the prosecution witnesses with an undying vigor. One by one, he paid his respects to each, bringing shame to a defense which in most eyes was despicable. He spoke of the evidence as being unreliable and unworthy and that if one link had to be molded or changed, it was a confession that there were inconsistencies in the prosecution's case.

Not withstanding his attack on the evidence, Mr. McGowan turned next to the purported motive. In his eyes there was no substantive motive that was adequate to drive his client to murder. To him it was incredulous that this woman who loved life could be driven to such a heinous act. To him there was "not a blot on her fair name, not a stain on her escutcheon" (*The Call*, December 30, 1898).

To Frank McGowan, John P. Dunning was little more than a worm. No woman who was associated with him would commit murder. John Dunning was mentally, morally, and physically an abomination. The woman accused of this heinous, immoral deed was his caretaker. She fed, clothed, and supported him through thick and thin. There was no cause for remorse, only rejoicing when Mr. Dunning took his leave. Frank McGowan, former senator from the great state of California, attacked and admonished all within his purview. From the most prominent to the most miniscule, no one escaped his wrath. To bear witness to this fact, McGowan noted that poor Maggie Smith of the Victoria Hotel was little more than a gaggle-eyed pop-walloper (*The Call,* December 30, 1898)).

Having castigated all that had dared testify against this fair maiden, McGowan closed his arguments by asking the jury:

> . . . not to cast a stain on the fair name of the accused woman's family (Brown). He warned them of the terrible penalty of their taking an innocent life and to spare the fair name of the State from an unjust verdict. . . . (*The Call,* December 9, 1898).

Frank McGowan had concluded the case for the defense with a self-serving indictment of the prosecution. The closing argument for the people was left to Mr. J. A. Hosmer. His effort was brilliant and some would say convincing to a fault. Neither stimulating in its rhetorical or oratorical points, it was a masterful analysis, however, of the testimony which had been presented in the case.

Mr. Hosmer's summation was cruel, pitiless, and scattered to the four winds the defense presented by Cordelia Botkin. The chief prosecutor, unlike Mr. Knight or Mr. McGowan, used cold, hard reasoning to thread together a compelling indictment of the accused. Circumstantial or direct evidence has but one premise; it could not be wholly absent. It was and forever would be the silent witness. Based upon a set of building blocks, the circumstantial case rested on a pyramid ranging from the simplistic to the complex.

John A. Hosmer on this day was indeed a man for which the defense had not reckoned. The defense case rested totally upon intimidation, supposition, and contradiction. He spoke of the defense attorney's poor taste in using scorn and ridicule instead of established fact. Honored by the largest attendance at the trial to date, he did not disappoint. As one wag remarked, it was well known that John A. Hosmer was the brains of the District Attorney's Office for the past ten years. On this day he lived up to the reputation.

J.A. Hosmer traced the case from its rudiments to the suspicion and arrest of Cordelia Botkin. At each point, he showed how the defense had erred in each of its contentions. He did not mitigate John Dunning's involvement in the sordid tale. Rather he explained from the date of the fateful meeting in Golden Gate Park, through years prior, to the death of Mary Elizabeth, Cordelia had a *motive*. She had a *means* by way of the mails, though the defense contended the package had never been mailed to commit the crime. Cordelia also had the *opportunity* by purchasing arsenic, candy, and the handkerchief and by her involvement in all the ancillary events in 1897. When considered in its totality, would Mrs. Ruoff, Miss Livernash or, for that matter, John Dunning coincidentally make the statements concerning Cordelia, if she were not involved? Considering the latter, would "Dunning come across the continent and open his lips and lay bare his past if he did not consider her guilty?" (*The Call*, December 31, 1898).

Those in doubt according to Mr. Hosmer need only consider the anonymous letters. Who else but Mrs. Botkin would be aware of details such as "financial difficulties," "race track speculation," and "both given to drink?" These were facts which only Cordelia would have had sufficient knowledge to incorporate into a letter. Consider also Almira Ruoff's testimony concerning the anonymous letters. Contained within the one letter was a solitary statement, "the bohemian life." Cordelia had admitted to its use in an interview given and printed in the *San Francisco Examiner* very early in the investigation. Almira had heard this reference on more than one occasion while in the presence of the accused.

In closing, J.A. Hosmer spoke to the jury of the gravity of the offense which had been committed. It was an offense which caused the deaths of two innocent women. The crime was premeditated and it was cowardly and it called for the supreme sacrifice. The gallows, and only the gallows, were the place for a person, man or woman, who was responsible for such a heinous and vile deed. With the conclusion of J.A. Hosmer's final summation to the jury, the court stood in recess as Judge Cook prepared his address prior to sending the jury into deliberations. Immediately after the recess was declared, a hum of conversation commenced within the courtroom. A hush did not return until the jury filed back into the courtroom.

Judge Carroll Cook commenced his formal charge to the jury, reciting those facts necessary for them to return a verdict of guilty or innocent against Cordelia Botkin. Having submitted points of law concerning certain disputed points, Cordelia's attorneys were confident as the judge made his presentation. Many points in their favor had been approved and now were included within his manuscript of jurisprudence. For her part, Cordelia was not so sure; her face took on an ashen hue and her lips twitched continuously. Moisture appeared at the edge of her eyes though, nary a tear fell. With the closing of the judge's charge, the jury filed from the courtroom to determine her fate. The time was five o'clock and there was no indication on the countenance of the twelve of what fate they would deliver.

At fourteen minutes past nine the courtroom bell broke the eerie silence of the night. Advised that a decision had been reached all gathered in expectancy of the verdict of innocent for Cordelia. The deliberations had been short and to the defense this could mean only a favorable outcome. Silence prevailed as the jury filed into their box. Asked if they had reached a verdict, foreman Kennedy answered in the affirmative. Having shown the verdict to Judge Cook, Kennedy was instructed to read it aloud. His words were of terrible impact and all, including Cordelia, sat in rapt attention.

> "We find," said Kennedy, "the defendant, Cordelia Botkin, guilty of murder in the first degree, and fix the punishment at imprisonment for the term of her natural life" (*San Francisco Examiner,* December 31, 1898).

As the verdict was read there was an audible "ah" from the crowd within the courtroom gallery. This was followed by stillness as the audience absorbed the impact of those few spoken words. There was no exultation, only a deep sadness for the fate which had befallen a fellow human being.

It had taken the jury only four hours and fourteen minutes to reach its decision. Cordelia Botkin, this modern day Lucretia Borgia who had mailed the box of arsenic laced bonbons, had been shown to be guilty by a remarkable web of circumstantial evidence.

Stoically sitting at the defense table, Cordelia's expression was sphinx-like. As the courtroom was cleared of the attendees who spoke in hushed tones, she gave no sign of what was innermost in her thoughts. As the jurors filed from their place within the courtroom, she peered upon each with defiant stare as if in disbelief.

George Knight, as was his duty, arose and addressed the judge as court went into recess. He offered his objections to the verdict and vowed that the defense would continue the fight. Later, he outlined the course which would be taken and vowed that "the verdict will fall." As Cordelia Botkin awaited transport back to the place which had for these longs months become her home, she gave in to her emotional distress and fainted. As water was brought and George Knight fanned her, she regained consciousness but not her composure. Looking squarely into Mr. Knight's eyes she blurted, "Why didn't you give me an American jury? I told you I wanted an American jury" (*San Francisco Examiner*, December 31, 1898).

Upon her return to the Branch County Jail, Cordelia Botkin had regained her brazen countenance and her powers of speech. In true Cordelia fashion she lashed out at those who had placed her in harm's way.

> The verdict was a greater surprise to me than I can make any one understand. I was confident that the jury would restore to me my freedom. My reason for this confidence was based on the testimony introduced during the trial. . . . I cannot but feel, and I think all thinking and intelligent people will agree with me, that in the verdict there is an entire absence of justice. . . . Is this our American justice to make me a woman a scapegoat? But, how ever shocked and disappointed I may be tonight, I am not discouraged. I yet feel that I shall be vindicated. The public will one day know that I am not the sort of woman this verdict of this jury would lead the people to believe. I can now do nothing but wait my time, trusting in a higher justice than was understood by the twelve men who were entrusted with the high duty of passing on a human life (*San Francisco Examiner,* December 31, 1898).

Abandoned by her husband Welcome A. from the time of her arrest in Stockton and abandoned by her son Beverly, Cordelia had but one avenue to shield herself from the storm. Her counsel, each in his own way, vowed to press the fight forward and not to desert her in these desperate hours.

Preparing to return east, the Delaware witnesses spoke briefly of the case, the trial, and the verdict. Joshua Deane was satisfied with the outcome but not overly elated for he had had reservations. Deane stated:

> The verdict was a surprise to me . . . for I had been led to believe from common report that it was impossible to convict a guilty person in San Francisco. This impression has been corrected. . . . I believe the verdict is in accordance with the testimony and evidence in the case, and am therefore satisfied (*San Francisco Examiner,* December 31, 1898).

Old John Pennington was his stoic self, always the gentleman, even after suffering the grievous loss of his daughters. The consummate attorney he spoke, but briefly, regarding his reaction:

> It would hardly be becoming in me to make any statement or voice any opinion in regard to the result of the trial, but I can say that I believe the jury has done its duty fairly and conscientiously. That is all I can say (*San Francisco Examiner,* December 31, 1898).

John P. Dunning, the paramour, the rake, and the person who had been instrumental in the entire sordid affair, spoke boldly and attempted to put this chaotic moment in some perspective:

> The only comment I care to make upon the verdict of guilty against Mrs. Botkin, is that it is certainly in accord with the testimony which I gave in the case myself. I have no feeling of exultation in the matter. . . . I knew before I came here the miserable, degrading story that I would have to tell, and I could have escaped it all by refusing to come. But I had no wish to shield the murderer of my wife. . . . From the first moment that I learned the circumstances attending the death of my wife and sister-in-law, I never had the shadow of a doubt as to who it was that caused the cruel murder. . . . I have been subjected to criticism of the virulent kind. . . . I will leave here as soon as possible, return to my old home, where this whole horrible story is told by two graves in the

little country church-yard, along the banks of the Delaware river. Then I will devote the remainder of my life to the happiness of all I have left, the little girl who bears on her face the imprint of her angel mother and who climbs upon my knee and asked me if her mamma has gone to heaven (*San Francisco Examiner,* December 31, 1898).

This said, the three major participants and the rest of the Delaware entourage boarded carriages for the distant journey east. All but John Dunning would travel together. Possibly feeling ostracized by his own actions, Mr. Dunning would wait an additional day prior to departure. Hoping that the California experience was behind them each in his own way fought to put the long separation from home and loved ones behind.

George Knight let all within earshot know that after the stormy events of the past weeks and through the welcome respite of a restful calm, another storm in the form of an appeal was on the horizon. With the sentencing of Cordelia Botkin, February 4, 1899, questions of jurisdiction and judicial misconduct would begin to burgeon into a full-fledged fight. The next few weeks and then successive years would bear out his words. Cordelia Botkin, temporarily removed from society, would not be forgotten. Time and time again she would rear her head and make her presence known.

Chapter Sixteen

She Will Appeal: Verdict Is Not in Keeping With the Law or Evidence

True to his vow to press forward, George Knight after the sentencing began his endeavor to secure Cordelia Botkin a new trial. He was a man of persistence if nothing else. The two major issues he attacked were that

> . . . neither Judge Cook, not any other Judge in the State of California had jurisdiction to try Mrs. Botkin . . . there is no law by which Mrs. Botkin can be extradited to Delaware. . . . It is simply a flaw in our legal system of which we shall take advantage (*San Francisco Bulletin,* December 31, 1898).

Mr. Knight's "fight for justice" would consume the greater portion of the next few years. Thwarted at all turns, the defense would press its issues through a variety of courts and finally take their arguments to the California Supreme Court, though the court stood firm in defiance to the questions posed by the defense regarding the decision. An interesting course of events totally unrelated to Cordelia Botkin was to bring success to her defenders.

A gentleman with the imposing name of Albert Frederick George Vereneseneckockockhoff (shortened, thank God, to Hoff for judicial purposes) had been tried for the murder of an odd-job woman in his employ. Hoff had been convicted of the crime by circumstantial evidence. The judge, Carroll Cook, had instructed the jury in his charge with the following statement: "Circumstantial evidence has the great advantage, that various circumstances from various sources are not likely to be fabricated" (*San Francisco Murders,* 1947).

In its ruling, regarding Judge Cook's charge, the California Supreme Court overturned the conviction with the following remarks:

> . . . whether or not circumstantial evidence is entitled to such credit or not, is a question to be determined by the jury for the evidence, and therefore the charge was plainly an argument for the prosecution, and in violation of . . . the Constitution, which provides . . . Judges shall not charge juries with the respect to matters of fact, but may state the testimony and declare the law" (*San Francisco Murders,* 1947).

Based on this short passage Cordelia Botkin became the recipient of a judicial gift. Hoff would be retried in 1900 and once again convicted. Entitled or not, the Botkin case would be remanded to the lower court for retrial. It would be four years hence, but Cordelia Botkin would have a second day in court.

The State of California which had been the burden of expense in the first trial at the cost of $ 20,000.00 plus would gather the force of justice and dip into its coffers once again. Having spent six years in jail Cordelia Botkin with all her flair would once again titillate the citizens of San Francisco and bring this infamous case to the forefront.

As the appeals had proceeded, Cordelia Botkin had been confined to the Branch County Jail in Ingleside. It was no doubt an ironic and fitting location for her incarceration. It was within walking distance of the Ingleside Race Track where she and her former lover John P. Dunning had spent many a gay and pleasurable afternoon.

Take care should you feel pity for the murderess convicted of the death of Mary E. Dunning. Cordelia and her attorneys would make the most of an event, though obscure at the time, which occurred on a warm, cloudless Sunday, on April 22, 1900. Judge Carroll Cook was a passenger on a trolley, which passed near the Branch County Jail.

He was returning from a visit to his wife's grave when he chanced to glance out the window. At the car stop one block from the Branch County Jail much to his unbelieving eyes, he saw Cordelia Botkin, the woman who he had sentenced, alight from the trolley and walk toward the jail. In the investigation which followed, the sheriff and his staff, all would contend that the judge was mistaken.

Cordelia would say little of the event but her defenders would bring forth the theory of the "other woman." This was the actual murderess, not Cordelia, who so closely resembled their client. She, this mysterious soul, was the real person who committed the heinous act in 1898 and was still on the streets of San Francisco. True or not, it did raise an interesting premise. Just over three years would pass, but as March 1904 approached, so did the time for Cordelia Botkin to face her fate once again. Having ruled the jail for six years with an iron fist, Cordelia was indeed an intimidating force. A private cell and all the comforts of home including the only free chair in the facility had bolstered her ego. Cordelia Botkin would persevere and not be intimidated by a society which could never comprehend a person of her self-worth.

Chapter Seventeen

Botkin defense Maligns Living and Dead to Account for Poisoning

The second trial of Cordelia Botkin for the malicious and premeditated murder of Mary Elizabeth Dunning commenced on schedule, March 9, 1904. Once again, the witnesses from Delaware would make the arduous trek across the country to testify. Substantially the same in number, twelve, most faces would be familiar, as would their names, but with two exceptions.

The stoic old gentleman and father of the victim, John B. Pennington had passed away in 1902. John P. Dunning's sister, Mary A. would replace him, and testify in his stead. Also missing would be Thomas Gooden, postmaster of Dover, who, due to illness, could not suffer the hardships of train travel. Elizabeth L. Kemp, a postal clerk in the Dover office, took his place.

Changes had also been made in the prosecutorial team which had worked so diligently to convict Cordelia Botkin in 1898. Mr. Lewis Byington replaced John A. Hosmer and was ably assisted by Judge Robert Ferral. They had worked feverishly for the past three months tightening the web of circumstances which had bound Mrs. Botkin to the case. Their efforts had been unrelenting, and despite minor setbacks such as the death and illness of witnesses, they felt their case was as strong as ever.

Across the aisle, the articulate and sometimes venomous, Mr. George Knight would once again be present for the defense.

Assisted again by Frank McGowan, Knight would once again attempt to save the woman who had "led a gay life and lived for pleasure." It was made clear to all present that the fight would be bitter. Eight days would be consumed to empanel a jury of twelve true and just men acceptable to the defense.

Arriving on March 17, the Delaware witnesses rested and awaited the beginnings of proceedings following the weekend. All were silent with one exception, Bernard J. McVey. A state detective at the time of the tragedy, he had since gone into private employment in Wilmington. Still the consummate police officer, he spoke matter of factly about the journey and the impending trial. A shade grayer than five years previous, he was the same imperturbably good-natured fellow.

He stated:

> We had a pleasant journey enough. We nearly ran into a fearful storm in Chicago, but happily, we escaped it. We are here now, and are prepared to do our utmost to bring Mrs. Botkin to justice. We have a stronger case, than before. . . . I am amused as well as surprised at one thing. . . . I hear the defense claims to have found an important witness in Coroner Wall. . . . I hear it is claimed that the verdict (at the inquest) was one of death from cholera morbus . . . Mr. Knight may have had a commissioner appointed to take Wall's evidence . . . but there is no truth . . . concerning the inquest and its results (*Every Evening,* March 18, 1904).

With jury selection completed, the trial of the *State of California v. Cordelia Botkin* (1904) was set to begin. The prosecution as in 1898 would have the burden of proof regarding the fateful events which began on August 9. Much of the testimony would be a restatement of facts presented during the first trial, but there would be some new and interesting revelations.

For the uneducated in criminal matters and to provide a sense of background regarding the criminal justice system, unless new avenues were explored in the second trial, witnesses were bound by their previous testimony. Unknown to the jury, the testimony given was much like a Hollywood script. Only new witnesses, should they appear, were allowed to answer questions extemporaneously. As an example of new witnesses, Miss Elizabeth Kemp, assistant to Postmaster Thomas Gooden, and Miss Mary A. Dunning were representative. Neither had testified at the first trial; therefore, any information they possessed was deemed virgin. Beyond this, the other Delaware witnesses, as well as the California witnesses, were allowed no variance.

Miss Elizabeth Kemp, representing the Dover Post Office, was for the prosecution a far better witness than her superior Thomas Gooden. It was she on the fateful day who removed the "mysterious package" from the mailbag and passed it to Mr. Gooden. Picking the package up she had remarked to Mr. Gooden that "Mrs. Dunning (at the Pennington house) was probably receiving a box of candy" (*San Francisco Examiner,* March 17, 1904). Whether women's intuition, or a person possessing psychic powers, Miss Kemp was indeed accurate.

The other new witness from Delaware was Miss Mary A. Dunning, sister of John P. Dunning. She was called to buttress the reading of the testimony of the now departed John B. Pennington. Not present when the box of candy was delivered, she arrived at the home before either of the women died. Miss Dunning was therefore, privy to all the events which transpired during their brief illness. She would provide a vital link regarding Dr. Bishop's ministrations, the subsequent deaths, and all steps taken by John B. Pennington concerning the disposition of the evidence in Delaware.

The trial, which was expected to take two weeks, began promptly at ten A.M., March 21, with the opening statement of Lewis Byington. A very articulate endeavor, Byington synopsized the prosecution's first presentation at the earlier trial. He then expounded upon the chain of circumstances, which the state would prove. At his closing, he hammered home the point that if all this was proven the state expected Cordelia Botkin to pay the ultimate price and "receive the uttermost limit of punishment."

This accomplished, the state began to lay the groundwork with the testimony of the Delawareans. Each in turn recounted the circumstances surrounding the course of events transpiring after the receipt of the mysterious package on August 9, six years previous. Their testimony was for the most part a rehashing of the tale of a diabolical and heinous act. One point elicited quite by accident surfaced during the testimony of Leila Deane, daughter of Ida Henrietta Deane. Vigorously opposed by George Knight, it never became part of the official record. While on the witness stand, Leila testified to a point concerning her deceased grandmother, Rebecca Pennington. Mrs. Pennington had partaken of one of the bonbons as the package was passed about the porch on that fateful evening. She had placed it in her mouth but quickly spat it out remarking that the candy was not very good.

Continuing with her recitation, Leila stated that the chocolate had fallen in the yard. A rabbit belonging to Mary Elizabeth Dunning, Elizabeth Dunning's little daughter, had chanced to nibble on it. The next morning, August 10, the rabbit was dead. Independent of any other fact, this would have substantiated the point that the candy was poisoned. Unfortunately as Miss Deane did not see the rabbit ingest the entire piece, the court disallowed this poignant circumstance.

Mr. Knight once again would attack the evening meal, which had consisted of trout, corn fritters, eggs, bread, and butter. Once again he would be thwarted by those who had partaken of the evening repast. Attacking all angles of the prosecution case, George Knight, this time, spared almost no one from his venomous assault. Fortunately he did spare Rosy, the Pennington's colored cook, and the pots and pans. The day closed with few new revelations beyond the incidental squabbling between the opposing attorneys.

The court convened, March 22, 1904, and received the testimony of the medicos, Dr. Lemuel Bishop and Dr. Presley Downes. Both gave factual testimony as to the victims' complaints and their treatment and diagnosis. Once again Dr. Bishop was vigorously attacked by Mr. Knight and the question of "cholera morbus" reared its ugly head. George Knight pounded at the two doctors with his inane questioning but made few inroads.

George Knight was in an extremely argumentative state and clashed with all that opposed his suppositions. He attacked Joshua Deane, the victim, Ida Henrietta Deane's husband, and pontificated about Professor Theodore Wolfe's analysis. His bravado to this point was unceasing and unrelenting. It was clear to all present within the standing room only courtroom that George Knight would follow any course which would benefit George Knight.

The defense pushed sensibility and courtroom ethics to the limit. Relentlessly badgered by Mr. Knight, Frank Grey was a prime example of the tactics employed. Six years after the first trial, he was once again asked to identify the defendant. Much was made of the fact that his response was, "To the best of my recollection it was she." Bullied and coerced by George Knight, Mr. Grey reluctantly admitted that humans could err " . . . and that it was not impossible for him to be mistaken." Smugly, George Knight released the witness from further cross-examination, totally satisfied by his ungentlemanly abuse.

As Mr. Knight was prone to say "there were bigger fish to fry." When court went into session, on March 23, he unleashed his newest theories as to who had really committed the crime. As was shown in the past, George Knight was indeed a man of preposterous theories. Just as he had in the first trial, George Knight once again shown he had no fear of using them. It was widely reported that on this day, George Knight's star had shone but in reality it was perhaps, another portion of his anatomy. Lewis Byington, Robert Ferral, the assemblage within the courtroom, and Judge Carroll Cook mustered all their willpower to restrain themselves in disbelief. George Knight with the pomposity of a ringmaster in the circus occupied the center ring.

Free with innuendo and insinuation, he intimated that Dr. Lemuel Bishop was the poisoner. Having misdiagnosed the cause of his patient's illness, he had administered arsenic to clear his conscience and remove the blot from his record. Having previously spared the cook, Rosy, George Knight redirected his course and accused her pots and pans once again of being responsible for the ptomaine poisoning which had extinguished two lives. This was followed by his reassertion that the copper kettles used by the Haas Candy Company had been tainted and therefore unbeknownst to anyone had transmitted the deadly poison into the candy partaken by the Doverites.

In the true tradition of an actor occupying center stage, he saved his most denigrating remarks for last. With total ambivalence he launched into a personal attack upon Chief of Police I. W. Lees, who was deceased. He charged that Lees, because of his own incompetence, had doped the candies given to Professor Thomas Price for analysis. This was done as asserted by George Knight because I. W. Lees had arrested an innocent person and knowing this now needed a scapegoat.

The sign of a good cop, even today, is how even after death the person can make a defense attorney squirm. Knowing that Chief Lees had been true to his profession, the gallery laughed heartily at George Knight's assertions and the prosecutors remained silent watching the jury and letting George Knight coil his own noose. All were taken back when Mr. Knight concluded his vindictive spewing with the statement "I feel as if I'd like to wash up after Lees . . . " (*San Francisco Examiner,* March 24, 1904).

Having verbally assaulted all the witnesses for the prosecution, which included Bernard J. McVey, George Haas and his employees, David Green and Mrs. G. W. Clarke (formerly Miss Kittie Dettner), George Knight felt contented. Through verbal abuse and outlandish assertions he had hoped to put doubts into the minds of the jurors. At the close of the day Lewis Byington, however, was to have the last word. He had let Mr. Knight "thunder" as Byington portrayed the defense attorney's bantering.

As the court recessed Lewis Byington stated:

> I was shocked by the declaration . . . against Chief of Police Lees. The accusation he makes against a dead man is indescribably horrible. . . . He can't prove one vestige of fact to support his charge. . . . Think of the enormity of his accusation. . . .The dead Chief of Police is charged with attempting a diabolical murder in plotting to have an innocent woman hanged . . . (he) has hurt his case by his rabid declaration (*San Francisco Chronicle,* March 24, 1904).

Chapter Eighteen

Women Throng the Courtroom at the Botkin Trial and Giggle Over Details of the Testimony

As George Knight was soon to find out, Lewis Byington and his co-counsel Robert Ferral in their prosecutorial effort were not to be mocked nor were they to take kindly to his abuse of witnesses.

Where Mr. Knight had shone so brightly the previous day, he was to fare badly, as did the entire defense, when court reconvened on March 24. A series of witnesses would take the starch from their tail and have a telling effect upon the defense's contentions. Confronted by the unflappable Almira Ruoff, the defense would once again be placed on the defensive. She retold the sordid tale of events which transpired in her presence and identified anonymous letters as being written without a doubt by Cordelia Botkin. She concluded her testimony by identifying the writing in the "With love to yourself and baby, Mrs. C" note.

With her direct knowledge of Cordelia Botkin's handwriting, Almira Ruoff stated, without hesitation:

> In my opinion what convinces me is the quotation marks made diagonally over the C are characteristic in her handwriting. I have frequently seen similar marks in her letters (*San Francisco Chronicle,* March 25, 1904).

Next to the witness stand was Dr. Thomas Stone, the physician who had treated Cordelia in Stockton on July 28, 1898. Playing a minor role for the prosecution in the first trial, he now expounded upon his famous conversation with Cordelia Botkin on that day.

> She asked me about arsenic. What size dose to give and how much would be fatal. She wanted to know how it tasted and I explained it had no taste. She wanted to know if too much of it would cause it to be vomited from the stomach. . . . I told her if I were going to end my life I would take morphine. I thought Mrs. Botkin was joshing and I was answering her in a joshing manner. She reverted a number of times to the subject of arsenic . . . (*San Francisco Chronicle,* March 25, 1904).

Reeling from the onslaught of such damming testimony, George Knight floundered through a number of minor witnesses. He proposed yet another theory of how the fatal arsenic came to be present in the candies. He intimated that Paris green, a poison used on strawberry plants and also used as a candy extract may have been the culprit. A representative from the George Haas Company, Henry Pape, soon laid this theory to rest. Paris green was not a component of any extract used by the company.

The last witness of the day was Mrs. Grace Twichler. As Miss Grace Harris in 1898, she had been George Knight's favorite aversion. Once again she testified that the defendant, Cordelia Botkin, was the purchaser of the handkerchief at the City of Paris. Her memory was still clear and precise. Cordelia Botkin resembled her dead mother. Once again Mr. George Knight, the non-chivalrous Victorian, attacked her with vengeance. He was not content until she was a tearful shell of her former self. As the day ended, it was clear to all that the defense had lost ground and would endure a long night awaiting the next onslaught.

As the day began, there was a sense of foreboding within the air from the defense, which was still regrouping from the events of the previous day. Like a damage control party on a sinking ship, they were to be pressed to the utmost. Attempting to deflect the prosecution George Knight continued with his theory of Paris green as the contaminate which had caused the misfortunate deaths. He intimated that the substance had been placed in the chocolate by this external source. Professor Thomas Price had taken the witness stand. Arduously tested to his credit he ignored this avenue as a probable cause of the arsenical poisoning.

George Knight who was unusually good-natured this day showed that the venomous viper was just below the surface. Relentlessly he attacked and rebuffed Mrs. Loretta Simpson, then W. W. Barnes, and finally William Rosello. None of the three had anything to gain from expressing their truthful thoughts, but this mattered little to George Knight. He then went toe to toe with John Dunnigan, the postal official, whose name was so close to Dunning. So vehement was George Knight in his denunciations, that at one point, Dunnigan rose from his chair in the witness box and many feared that fisticuffs might ensue. The judge with a cool head diffused the situation and John Dunnigan was released.

The final portion of the day took on a much calmer air, but the portent of disaster was on the horizon for the defense or so it seemed. The last witness of the day was to be a fireman employed by the City of San Francisco. It was the prosecution's contention that he would provide the "missing link" in, as Lewis Byington acclaimed, a very strong case.

His name is unknown to us to this day. As the trial transcripts and other sustaining information were destroyed in 1906, we know little else. It appears that the defense may have been successful in its endeavor to exclude his testimony. However, in the interest of presenting an unbiased rendition of the case, it is presented, synopsized as a postscript to the trial.

The *San Francisco Examiner,* March 25, 1904, reported:

> He is a young man and former soldier, having served as a volunteer and then as a regular in the Philippine Islands. It was on July 31, 1898, that fateful Sunday . . . accompanied by a young woman, he was going to Oakland to say goodbye to friends. . . . When he reached the Phelan Building he stepped into the George Haas Store. . . . As he walked to the counter, he noticed a rather stout, somewhat showy woman who then and there purchased chocolate cream candies. He noticed her because of her manner. . . . He thought she was a very vain woman . . . with whom an acquaintance could be struck up on very slight provocation. . . . He made his own purchase and left. The young man did as most young men do when they are a long way from home–he read every scrap of news in the San Francisco papers and soon became

> interested in every detail of the web woven around Cordelia Botkin. . . . The sale of the chocolates impressed him . . . then like a flash it came upon him that the woman he saw that afternoon . . . might be Cordelia Botkin . . . he never thought to let the police know . . . the trial was over and the woman has been sentenced to life imprisonment. . . . In the meantime . . . a new trial had been granted (home from the war and now a fireman) . . . he was curious and went to the courthouse. . . . One good look at her was sufficient for she had changed but little in the years. . . .

This said, the case against Cordelia Botkin embarked on a two-day hiatus as the weekend approached.

Boisterous as the defense had been at the outset, they were now quite reticent and quietly retired to lick their wounds. Hopes for a quiet weekend were to be dashed on Sunday, March 27. Cordelia Botkin who had been strangely quiet during the first week of the trial was about to make her presence or non-presence known.

At Grace Church, on this Sunday, a heavily veiled woman was to appear. Resembling Mrs. Botkin, the assumption was that her long lost double had once again appeared. When confronted with this fact, Cordelia, as only she could do, denied all accusation. Her response was that of surprise.

> I have not been out of the county jail today and I do not understand how such a rumor could have been started. I have heard it circulated around town that I attended Grace Church this morning, but there is absolutely no truth in the report (*San Francisco Examiner,* March 28, 1904).

Also flatly denying any complicity was the Superintendent of the Branch County Jail. "There was no necessity to go down to church as we have service here every Sunday" (*San Francisco Examiner,* March 28, 1904).

Speculation therefore arose that Cordelia Botkin had a double. Remember back to 1900 when Judge Cook on his famous trolley ride, had brought accusations against the jail for allowing the incarcerated Cordelia free reign to the city. In truth, however, consider the fact that Lizzie Borden while awaiting trial was allowed to trek around Fall River. It was the sign of an age, how else could it be explained? Poor Frank McGowan would attempt during the ensuing weeks of the trial to locate "the double," but with no success. Probability says she did not exist, but Cordelia to her credit had struck once again.

That aside, the trial of Cordelia Botkin recommenced on Monday morning, March 28, 1904. The prosecution's star witness, John P. Dunning, and the experts in handwriting analysis would consume the ensuing two days. Once again John Dunning would espouse his sordid tale of this extramarital affair and the deceit which accompanied it. Unlike the first trial though, he would endure the pain of innuendo; the defense was far less rigorous in its attacks. It seemed that Mr. Dunning and his sordid tale of infidelity would be minimized. The defense had apparently decided to acquiesce to the facts surrounding this sordid liaison.

Identification of known handwriting samples of Cordelia Botkin and their comparison to the anonymous letters was accepted from the expert with little fanfare. There were few points of contention ensuing from the testimony on Monday and Tuesday. First Theodore Kytka had testified and Daniel Ames followed him. Both were in concert that the anonymous handwriting and Cordelia Botkin's were without doubt from the same hand. In the interim between their testimony and John Dunning, poor Maggie Smith, the cook at the Victoria Hotel, William Raymond, and Julius Ray had testified.

Rattled as she was, Maggie could not be diswayed from a poignant point of fact. She had seen Mrs. Botkin returning from an outing the day she was supposed to be prone with illness. Following her to the witness stand was Mr. Raymond and Mr. Ray. They together provided much more damming testimony. Employed at the City of Paris as cashiers in 1898, both testified that Mrs. Botkin cashed money orders in their presence and therefore had been a frequent patron of the store.

Cordelia at this point leaned toward George Knight and in a voice clearly audible to the court and all present stated "was that my double?" George Knight must have cringed at this disrespect for the criminal justice system. It was pure Cordelia, the consummate showgirl who even in this time of dire stress managed to exhibit impish bravado and theatrical flamboyance.

Expectations were high that the prosecution would conclude its presentation of the chain of evidence on March 29 and rest its case. With the tying of a few loose ends, the prosecution would adjure to the defense and the trial would enter its final phase. It was thought that the most spectacular event would be the star of the proceeding, Cordelia Botkin. All present were wrong as the following three days would be rift with controversy from a totally unexpected source.

Jacob Goetjen, one of the jurors in the case, stepped forward casually and announced he had been approached and offered fifty dollars to hang the jury. In the melee which followed, the defense accused the prosecution, the prosecution accused the judge, and Cordelia sat in disbelief. Three agonizing days would be consumed in an attempt to rectify a very peculiar situation.

It was indeed perplexing for Judge Cook who faced an aberration which no justice need encounter. George Knight moved immediately for a declaration of a mistrial, the dismissal of the present jury, and a new jury summoned. Having already placed on call twenty-five hundred talisman and having begun a major trial, where would twelve, true, and just men be located?

Biting closely at Mr. Knight's heels was the prosecutor, Lewis Byington. His argument, which amounted to a tirade, was totally opposite to a mistrial. He placed the full emphasis for this debacle upon the shoulders of Judge Carroll Cook. Three days of indecision would ensue, but the Judge's vacillation was no doubt heavy upon his mind. The question remained which direction should he go? A mistrial would forgo the defense any opportunity of appeal through exception. Conversely, the reaction of the prosecution and the entire legal community could bring condemnation upon him. Faced by the dilemma, the justice, as most justices will, took an inordinate amount of time and did nothing. Cornered, by both sides as the days wore by endlessly, he was finally forced to make a decision.

On March 31, while Judge Cook was preparing to declare a mistrial a resolution materialized and it was from a most unlikely source. On that day, Cordelia Botkin dictated the following statement, which was presented to the court.

> I passed through two terrible ordeals in selecting juries and I do not believe that I could ever go through a similar experience. I have entirely satisfied myself that this jury will render me a just and fair verdict. . . . After six years isolation it was a terrible thing to be thrust into the world again and to be compelled to select twelve men to pass upon my life. And now for the coming results I can only offer constant prayer that these men will render a just verdict and through it vindicate an innocent woman (*San Francisco Examiner,* April 1, 1904).

Acquiescing to their client, George Knight and Frank McGowan with reluctance accepted Cordelia's decision. Her plea to continue was duly recorded. The prosecution, defense, and the court agreed upon minor points of law and upon resolution of these factors, Lewis Byington rested his case. The trial was set to resume the following day with presentation of Cordelia's defense.

Chapter Nineteen

Mrs. Botkin on Witness Stand and Refutes Some of the More Important Testimony for the Prosecution

Court proceedings commenced on schedule, April 1, 1904, with the defense calling its primary witness, Cordelia Botkin, to the stand. There was without doubt a sense of irony in the date upon which she testified. Cynics would probably find it amusing that "April Fools Day" was an appropriate date for the court to receive her testimony. She set the stage for the course of events in her direct testimony as she answered George Knight's question.

From the outset Cordelia wove a tale once again of total deniability and of an innocent woman persecuted by the criminal justice system. Nervous at first, she warmed to the occasion as Mr. Knight unerringly led her through a circuitous odyssey of the life and times of Cordelia Botkin. She was as on the previous occasion a very good witness for herself.

Her answers were all well rehearsed and point by point she gave answers which were diametrically opposed to the prosecution's circumstantial chain of evidence. Cordelia told of the chance meeting with John Dunning in Golden Gate Park, on that fateful day, many years previous. She spoke of the friendship which ensued and how she assisted him financially when he was downtrodden. There was nothing other than a platonic relationship between them. Intimacy never entered her mind as she poignantly stated she was a married woman. She told of her movements to the numerous sites within the city which culminated in her residency at the Victoria Hotel. Cordelia spoke of travel and of her numerous ventures to the north to visit friends and relatives. She specifically attacked the prosecution's witnesses, making a clean sweep with denial after denial. Cordelia declared that she had never been in the George Haas Candy Store. As to arsenic, she refuted having ever purchased it in lump or powdered form. Cordelia disavowed the purchase of the handkerchief at the City of Paris which had been placed in the candy box.

As the morning moved ever onward, Cordelia focused on the writing evidence. She disclaimed the authorship of the "With love to yourself and baby" note and the writings on the wrapper. This was followed by a strong repudiation as the author of the anonymous letters. As to Miss Lizzie Livernash and Almira Ruoff, she regarded both with disdain. The first was mistaken in all that she had reported. Conversations had taken place in Livernash's presence, but she had misrepresented them.

The latter person, Mrs. Almira Ruoff, was much like John Dunning, an ungrateful and bitter person. Cordelia challenged most conversations between her and Almira, branding them mostly, as figments of Ruoff's furtive imagination. Regarding Dr. Thomas Stone, she denied conversing with him on the subject of poison, specifically arsenic.

Loquacious in her manner, Cordelia sprang one surprise on all present. Having categorically denied every material allegation made by the prosecution, she referenced one of the anonymous letters. She claimed that the state's exhibits was not an original but a clever copy made by a member of the Pennington family, perhaps even John B. Pennington himself. She knew this for a fact as John Dunning had forwarded the original to her for her perusal. His wife had sent this letter to John P. in 1897 and, therefore the state could not possibly have the original. No less surprised by this statement was George Knight who must have regretted at this point the loose cannon he had unsecured. As to the whereabouts of this original document now alas Cordelia stated she had destroyed it.

Having taking a course of total denial, Cordelia had the presence of mind to attempt to once again shift suspicion from herself. Mrs. Corbalay's name once again entered the proceedings as the infamous "Mrs. C." If nothing else, Cordelia was a woman who could think on her feet. In closing his direct examination, George Knight took one last parting shot at the court and at the prosecution. Still attempting to locate Cordelia's elusive *double,* he asked Cordelia, "On April 22, 1900, did you alight from streetcar in San Francisco?" An emphatic "No" was Cordelia's response. The defense concluded its direct examination at this point and awaited the onslaught from the prosecution.

Cordelia Botkin would endure a long afternoon this day, and some would say, survive unscathed. Others would be less kind in their remarks. Cordelia had for her part forgotten a vital point as she testified this second time. A transcript from the first trial existed, and many of her former statements were contradictory to her present contentions.

Lewis Byington was not John A. Hosmer, and he went after Cordelia Botkin relentlessly. Beginning slowly, Byington asked a few inconsequential, perfunctory questions. Having set the stage, he pushed forward with questions regarding Cordelia's relationship with Mr. Dunning. Through contradiction after contradiction, Byington was able to show that their liaisons were anything but platonic. The trap laid by Lewis Byington was masterful. Having testified at the first trial that Dunning's wife and child were staying in Dover, Cordelia now announced that she was unsure whether it was Dover or Philadelphia. It was with great reluctance that she admitted that her memory might be faulty.

Rather than continue with outright contradictions of these facts presented, Cordelia now charted a new course. To questions concerning her conversations with Lizzie Livernash and Almira Ruoff, she said that both had misconstrued the facts plain and simple. To accentuate this point, Cordelia testified in response to a question from George Knight:

> I was unconscious for hours and was not responsible for all the statements Miss Livernash says I made. I have absolutely no recollection of declaring, 'Oh, why did I not let the man die and spare the mother to his child.' If I said that it was the vagary of a disordered mind (*The Call,* April 2, 1904).

Why she was asked would Mrs. Ruoff misconstrue things she had witnessed? To this Cordelia cynically responded, "To fit her testimony."

Cordelia was having a very difficult and uneasy time under Lewis Byington's tenacious assault. Frequently she gave responses which were unlike her previous testimony. When her former depositions were then read into the record, she would with great reluctance recant and admit their correctness. Cordelia was not a person to give into defeat, and as fact after fact was elicited, she made strides to adjust the variance of the past to fit the present. She was if nothing audacious. Having been identified in court by Frank Grey, Cordelia denied ever having met the man or for that matter ever having been in the Owl Drug Store.

Though it would be up to a jury of her peers to decide upon guilt or innocence, Cordelia had been bruised and battered by her ordeal. She was released from further testimony and sought refuge at her attorney's side. The defense requested a recess to the following Monday with hopes that the presentation of its case would conclude quickly on that date. The court and the prosecution posed no opposition to this request. However, prior to proceedings ending for the week, it was suggested that the long awaited deposition of the former Dover Coroner William Walls, be read into the record. Contrary to what the defense, had contended, the coroner had signed the death certificates much to their chagrin. He had, in fact, noted the cause of death: "Arsenical Poisoning."

With this accomplished the court recessed and Frank McGowan began his ever-vigilant quest once again in hopes of locating Cordelia's ever-elusive double. Cordelia having regained her composure brought the day to a close with some final remarks:

> I am resting strongly in the hope that the court and the world will recognize the wonderful revelation the prosecution gave me the opportunity to make in regard to the last original anonymous letter and its copy . . . This is a sample of the Delaware evidence against me. It is quite in line with the Coroner's Inquest. The autopsy on that occasion having been performed on the box of candy instead of the bodies of the deceased women (*San Francisco Examiner,* April 2, 1904).

A quiet weekend prevailed as the trial, having reached its apex, prepared to enter its final phase. With Monday came the conclusion of the defense case as Cordelia's attorneys attempted to interject some form of doubt. The final witnesses were presented to show that Cordelia should be vindicated for a variety of reasons.

The first witness was former Sheriff John Lackman who testified that Cordelia was incarcerated on April 22, 1900, and therefore could not have been the mysterious woman seen by Judge Cook alighting from the streetcar. William Speagle followed him to the witness box. His purpose was to give testimony concerning the sailing times of steamers which traveled daily from the Port of San Francisco. Mr. Speagle was a newspaperman in Eureka and his paper listed the daily schedule for these ships. The defense contended that Cordelia could not have been the author of the San Francisco posted anonymous letters, for Speagle showed that she was in Eureka, fifty miles up the coast. Speagle's wife next was called to testify and related that she had met Mrs. Botkin at a card party in Eureka, June of 1897. Each person called, and these included J. H. Walkington of the City of Paris and Thomas Ford, Superintendent of Mails for San Francisco, was presented for one purpose. The purpose was clear from the standpoint of the defense, muddy the waters. Once again, the defense presented the poor hapless doctor, George Tyrrell.

The intent here was to show that the doctor had ministered to an ailing Cordelia Botkin on July 31, 1898, in her rooms at the Victoria Hotel. Once again due to his own ineptitude, Dr. George Tyrrell was broasted like a chicken on a spit by the prosecution. Passed over the previous day with a simple acknowledgement, the defense introduced the deposition by William Walls. With this accomplished George Knight rested the case for the defense.

As the court adjourned for the day, Judge Cook announced to the adversarial attorneys that each would have one session of court on Tuesday afternoon, Wednesday, and Thursday morning for their closing remarks. This said they went into adjournment until ten A.M. the following day. Leaving court, Lewis Byington enlightened all within hearing distance of an alternative avenue the State would pursue against Cordelia Botkin should she be found not guilty.

With little or no fanfare, Mr. Byington announced that if by some happenstance Cordelia Botkin were acquitted, she would not go free. It was the State's intention that should they fail to convict her for the murder of Mary Elizabeth Dunning, she would be charged with the murder of Ida Henrietta Deane. Byington made the following statement regarding this from the courthouse steps:

> Yes, I am considering my course in case the present charge against Mrs. Botkin should fail either by reason of acquittal or disagreement of the jury. In either of these events we shall proceed to try Mrs. Botkin for the murder of Mrs. Deane . . . (*San Francisco Examiner,* April 5, 1904).

With this announcement, he retired to prepare for the summations and forge ahead with the present endeavor. Both the defense attorneys and Cordelia were strangely silent. The former, anticipating this event, kept its countenance to itself. For Cordelia the words must have held a portent of pending gloom, and for once she was speechless.

Chapter Twenty

Woman's Fate Will Be in the Hands of the Jury

The closing summations were long and arduous as both sides sought to find favor with the jury. Short extracts from the speeches of Judge Robert Ferral for the prosecution and George Knight for the defense are presented herein. They provide the essence of the views expounded by the opposing sides during the two days which followed.

Judge Robert Ferral speaking for the prosecution stated harshly and with little remorse:

> This was a woman's crime, I am ashamed to say. There is no record of a man ever having sent poisoned candy to work destruction of life . . . I can see Chief Lees as he sat in his office thinking, thinking, thinking. He had come to one conclusion it was a woman's crime. . . . What kind of a woman should he be looking for? A woman who was abandoned to all instincts of motherhood; one who was altogether gone to vice and depravity. . . . Did he find such a woman? Yes, he found her in Cordelia Botkin. . . . This woman is a female Frankenstein; she is without heart, without feeling, without conscience–a monster. . . . The grave responsibility is upon you to uphold law and justice, intelligently, honestly, and bravely though the course may lead to the gallows . . . (*San Francisco Chronicle,* April 6, 1904).

With these remarks, Judge Ferral concluded, and Mr. George Knight rose from his chair to enter the heated debate. As an orator, he was second to none. On this day, with all the eloquence he could muster, George Knight made an impassioned plea for the acquittal of Cordelia Botkin. George Knight attacked the prosecution's case of circumstantial fact from all sides. To him the evidence presented was little more than a paper tiger holding little or no weight.

The prosecution's case to George Knight was placed purely on conjecture, inadequate investigation, suspicious evidence, and faulty identifications. Concluding his remarks George Knight stated:

> Before God: I believe in my heart she is innocent, and I would be willing to try this case before twelve judges who are trained to weigh the evidence and decide upon it. . . . If there is a reasonable doubt in this case you've got to give it to Mrs. Botkin by an acquittal. . . . All that we ask is that you will guard this human life and this human liberty as you guard your twenty dollar gold piece and this woman will be free. I ask at your hand for Mrs. Botkin's' acquittal in view of the testimony in this case (*San Francisco Chronicle,* April 6, 1904).

A sense of expectation filled the air as all present realized that the *State of California v Cordelia Botkin* was about to come to a close. The last speaker in the case was District Attorney Lewis Byington. He began his closing remarks thusly:

> I agree with Mr. Knight; we want you gentlemen to try this case according to the law of this State and evidence of the witnesses. It is not a question of Mr. Knight's personality. . . . (*The Call,* April 8, 1904).

With those words spoken, Byington held the gathered crowd spellbound as he launched into the proof of guilt in glowing detail.

Following a set course, Lewis Byington without shouting, ranting, or melodrama pointedly recapitulated the state's case. Pounding home point after point of why the prosecution felt the web of circumstance led to Cordelia's door, he suddenly paused. Dramatically, he then reiterated the defendant's own testimony and her contradictions of the events which had transpired. As he closed his recitation Lewis Byington beseeched the jury:

> If this defendant is found guilty of murder in the first-degree mete but to her the full penalty of the law. Before the dawn of civilization your God and my God on Mount Sinai said, Thou shalt not kill. . . . (*The Call,* April 8, 1904).

Having completed his soliloquy, Mr. Byington resumed his seat and awaited the court's charge to the jury.

To Judge Cook's credit, his charge to those who would decide the fate of Cordelia Botkin was tempered. Perhaps he remembered the Supreme Court's ruling in his prior decisions, or perhaps he wanted to be slow and methodical to give Cordelia every benefit for acquittal by "reasonable doubt." If nothing else, the legal community and the attorneys present for both sides could not fault his fairness. At the end of his charge, Judge Cook took special note of circumstantial evidence and carefully instructed the jury of its weight, following the mandate of the higher court. At the close of his lengthy charge to the jury, the court recessed while they retired to deliberate. The time was 4:27 P.M.

Several times during the late afternoon, the jury requested items of evidence and testimony to be reread. They were, despite the pale of the bribery insinuation, conscientious. At 11:15 P.M., a little under seven hours after retiring to deliberate, the court was informed that a verdict had been reached. The moment of truth was upon Cordelia Botkin.

Stoically the jurors filed one by one into the jury box for the last time. After what seemed like an eternity, Judge Cook spoke, "Gentlemen of the jury have you agreed upon a verdict?" The foreman, Morris Hyman in a firm and deliberate voice responded, "We have, your Honor" and handed the slip of paper to the clerk of the court (*The Call,* April 8, 1904). Judge Cook after reviewing the verdict instructed the clerk to read aloud the jury's verdict. In an unimpassioned tone the clerk read these words and the die was cast.

> We the jury find the defendant, Cordelia Botkin guilty of murder in the first degree and fix and access her punishment therefore at imprisonment in the State prison for life (*The Call,* April 8, 1904).

A hushed silence prevailed in the court, and with this the jury had spoken. The judge thanked each jury member for their diligence in the matter, released them from their duty, and set the date of sentencing for April 16. The immediate and expected response from George Knight was almost instantaneous with the verdict. He said:

> We shall appeal of course we shall appeal. The Supreme Court will never sustain a verdict such as that. The jury did not have the evidence upon which to convict. Mrs. Botkin should have been set free. I say the Supreme Court will set the verdict aside. It is unjust (*San Francisco Examiner,* April 8, 1904).

Lewis Byington spoke in response for the prosecution and the people.

> I am, he said, well satisfied with the verdict of the jury and while I worked hard and expected a verdict of hanging . . . I am of the opinion that ample justice had been done. . . . The defense may appeal the case to the Supreme Court but I am positive the appeal will be fruitless. . . . The verdict is a just one and a triumph for the people (*The Call,* April 8, 1904).

Cordelia had received the verdict with a sense of stoicism. Neither tear nor tremor of emotion showed upon her person. Gallant and pompous to the end, Cordelia Botkin turned to the crowd and sneered at them with disdain as she left the courtroom. She bade a fond goodbye to her sister Mrs. McClure. Her only statement had been to her attorneys George Knight and Frank McGowan. Immediately after the verdict was read she had announced:

> You held out too much encouragement to me. I am resigned to my fate. I never expect to be granted another trial. You have been too good to me. It is my fate (*The Call,* April 8, 1904).

Epilogue

Death Puts End To Sentence Of Mrs. Botkin

If Cordelia Botkin had a sense that her trials and tribulations were at an end, she was sadly mistaken. While the jury listened to closing statements in the court proceedings, just completed, another legal crises was taking shape in another portion of the courthouse. Unbeknownst to anyone, Joshua Deane was swearing to a complaint, which charged Cordelia Botkin with the murder of his wife, Ida Henrietta.

Long months would follow as once again the wheels of justice would churn into motion. Haggard and to the point of exhaustion, Cordelia's attorneys would fight a battle on two fronts. First was the lengthy appeal through the courts, culminating in a hearing before the California Supreme Court which would fall on deaf ears.

Cordelia's attorneys argued long and laboriously for a reversal of the decision, citing error upon error, and noting relevant points of jurisprudence which would sustain their plea. With all hope vanishing, George Knight referenced the case of Florence Maybrick wrongly accused in the death of her husband, James Maybrick. Released from prison after fifteen years, it had been shown that Mrs. Maybrick was the victim of a system, which had rushed to judgment.

All was for naught. The justices of the Supreme Court refused to accommodate Mr. Knight's suggestion, as to their mind the Maybrick case had no bearing in regards to the Botkin case.

Without just cause or precedent, Mr. Knight was to forgo a further battle in this arena.

Concerning the second front, the defense was far more successful. They argued that Cordelia's rights had been violated as she was entitled "to a speedy trial." Six years had passed since her arrest for the death of Mary E. Dunning and thus a speedy trial had been placed beyond question. From the sentencing which occurred on April 16, 1904, to November 29, 1904, the state pressed forward its demands that she be tried for Ida Henrietta's death.

The Delaware witnesses had to be detained and their depositions duly taken. Cordelia Botkin faced with insurmountable odds had lost all semblance of herself and seemed resigned to her fate. It is unknown if there was a change of heart or if the thought of the expense of a third trial was engendered in the minds of those in power, but Cordelia would not stand trial. Whatever the reason perhaps it was the certainty that Cordelia was already facing life imprisonment. Having accomplished its primary goal, the State of California acquiesced and rescinded its demand for justice. The knowledge that she had killed Mary Dunning and thus, if this was true, did kill Ida H. Deane may have been satisfactory to the California bureaucrats.

Cordelia Botkin was prostrate with grief and seized by melancholy. Removed from society, she appeared to have resigned herself to the outcome. Cordelia however was not one to abdicate that easily and in one last-ditch effort during the month of February 1910, she sought clemency and parole from the governor of California. She based this final appeal on the fact that she was suffering from ill health. The loss of her beloved son Beverly, who died in 1909 had brought her to a point of despondency and left her a helpless invalid. Turning a deaf ear, the Appellate Court denied Cordelia's request which they felt lacked merit. Having been transferred to San Quentin Penitentiary, May 16, 1906, after the San Francisco Earthquake, Cordelia lost all hope of freedom.

On March 7, 1910, after suffering a nervous breakdown, she died at 9:30 P.M. The cause of death was listed as softening of the brain due to melancholy. Her former lover and paramour John P. Dunning had preceded her in death by three years. His death came April 17, 1907, in Philadelphia, and the cause was cerebral hemorrhage. With Cordelia Botkin's death, the last chapter was written in a story of love, intrigue, and, murder. Her sensational trials had electrified the country for just over a decade. To her credit, Cordelia fought through every legal channel available, from the time of her arrest to her death.

She never admitted her guilt as either a participant or an accomplice. From her death bed she protested her innocence and stated:

> I wish to die as there is nothing left for me. I am being punished for the deed of another (*San Francisco Chronicle,* March 8, 1910).

The consummate actress to the end, Cordelia Botkin has left us all her legacy to interpret.

Appendix I

The Poem

Cordelia Botkin took a box
and filled it up with
poisoned chocolates.

She mailed it East
so it is said
And, now, two Dover women
are dead.

–Anonymous

Appendix II

Fingerprints as Evidence

Today we take fingerprints for granted. Each human being, as books, television, and the movies tell us, has ten distinct prints on his fingers, which make our person identifiable as an individual. The classic line "ten points makes you a liar" is now an indelible part of our criminal justice system and, for that matter, our culture.

The obvious question, then, one may ask, is why didn't John Pennington and the State Detectives, in 1898, have the candy wrapper and the letter within examined for this valuable clue? No more tell-tale sign of the murderer could have been found. Imagine what Cordelia Botkin, or one of the other women she accused, faces when confronted with this incontrovertible evidence.

For that matter consider Lizzie Borden, or a multitude of other murderers, being faced with this prospect. Unfortunately, this was a fantasy in the nineteenth century. Though a monumental advancement for mankind, fingerprints and identification by this means, was only in its infancy.

The first conviction based on fingerprint evidence would not take place in the United States until 1911. This was approximately one year after the death of Cordelia Botkin and would have been meaningless to the criminal justice system.

Life, as they say, is based on "what ifs," and the results of an examination of the evidence would today be inconsequential. Circumstantial evidence allowed Cordelia to escape with her life. Direct evidence, in the form of fingerprints, would have doomed her to the short end of a very long rope.

Appendix III

Jurors Names and Addresses
Of the 1898 and 1904 Trial
In
State of California v. Cordelia Botkin

December 1898 Jurors

Abe Jacobs	212 Leavenworth Street
Willard B. Hamington	1118 Sacramento Street
John F. Myer	16 Alpine Street
Jacob Heyman	2705 California Street
Edward A. Keil	2528 Mission Street
J. H. Burns	3347 17th Street
T. H. Chandler	911 Polk Street
A. E. Buckingham	2806 Jackson Street
J. F. Kennedy	1727 Pine Street
S. K. Overgaard	1001 Pine Street
S. H. Daniels	1821 Leavenworth Street
M. Marcuse	1724 Santa Clara Avenue Almeda

April 1904 Jurors

William S. McDevitt	4022 22nd Street
Vernon Lipton	205 Presidio Avenue
Jacob Goetjen	249 5th Street
Julius Lilenthal	307 Fulton Street
Morris Hyman	2230 Sacremento Street
Henry Peters	87 S. Broderick Street
Bernard Wambold	732 Ivy Avenue
Ferdinand Salz	1630 Haught Street
James H. Robertson	503 Capp Street
William M. O'Connor	Hotel Street Dunston
S. P. Robbins	622 Turk Street
John P. Carroll	14 Lake Street

Appendix IV

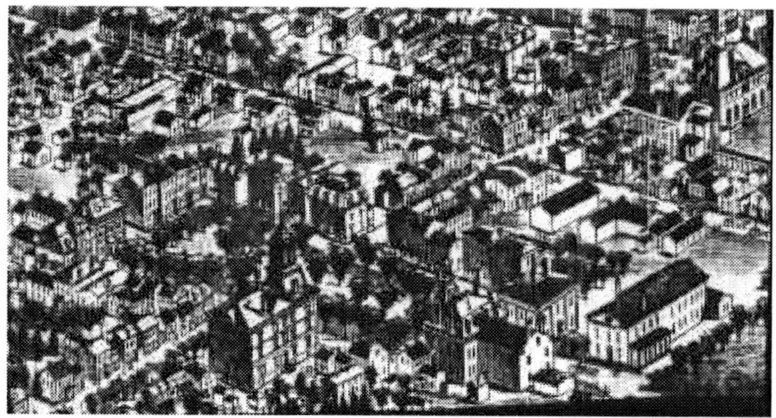

Dover Green showing the home of John Pennington and little Harry's route to the Post Office.
Author's collection

The residence of John B. Pennington. circa 1900
Courtesy of Delaware State Archives

George Haas Candy Store, 810 Market Street in San Francisco
(5th Awning from the corner)
Courtesy of San Francisco History Center
San Francisco Library

Owl Drug Store, 1128 Market Street in San Francisco
(just below the Dry Goods sign)
Courtesy of San Francisco History Center
San Francisco Library

City of Paris Dry Goods, Union Square San Francisco (now Neiman Marcus) circa 1897
Courtesy of San Francisco History Center
San Francisco Library

Victoria Hotel, California and Hyde Streets San Francisco
Courtesy of San Francisco History Center
San Francisco Library

Dunning, Mary Elizabeth

STATE OF DELAWARE.

Certificate of a Death.

In the State of Delaware Kent County.

IF AN INFANT, NOT NAMED, GIVE PARENT'S NAME.

Full name of deceased Mary Elizabeth Dunning

Age 35 years *Color* white

Nation or State Delaware

If of foreign birth, how long in the United States.

Residence Dover

Occupation

~~Single~~, married, ~~widowed~~. (Cross out words not required in this line)

Sex Female

Name and Nation of Parents Delawarean

Cause of death and complications Arsenic Poison sent by U S mail by parties unknown

Date of death Aug 12/98

I Hereby Report *this death, and certify that the foregoing statements are true, according to the best of my knowledge.*

Witness my hand this 17th *day of* Aug 1898

Signature and residence of reporter. [illegible]
Coroner

Returned *to the Recorder of Deeds of Kent Co.*

189...... *by* ...... *Undertaker,*

residing at ...... W. L. PRITCHETT, UNDERTAKER & EMBALMER, *in Kent County.*

Signed, DOVER, DEL.

Death Certificate for Mary Elizabeth Dunning showing the cause of death
Courtesy of Delaware State Archives

Dean, Ida H.

STATE OF DELAWARE.

Certificate of a Death.

In the State of Delaware Kent County.

IF AN INFANT, NOT NAMED, GIVE PARENTS' NAME.

Full name of deceased Mrs Ida H. Dean

Age 44 years *Color* white

Nation or State Delaware

If of foreign birth, how long in the United States.

Residence Dover

Occupation

~~*Single*~~, *married*, ~~*widowed*~~. (Cross out words not required in this line)

Sex Female

Name and Nation of Parents Delawarean

Cause of death and complications Arsenic Poison Sent by U S mail by parties unknown

Date of death Aug 11/98

I Hereby Report *this death, and certify that the foregoing statements are true, according to the best of my knowledge.*

Witness my hand this 17th *day of* Aug 1898

Signature and residence of reporter. W D Walls Coroner

Returned *to the Recorder of Deeds of Kent Co.*

189 *by* W. L. PRITCHETT, *Undertaker,*

residing at UNDERTAKER & EMBALMER, DOVER, DEL. *Kent County.*

Signed,

Death Certificate of Ida Henrietta Deane
Courtesy of Delaware State Archives

Photograph of the Victim,
Mary Elizabeth Dunning
Courtesy of the San Francisco Examiner

Photograph of Ida Henrietta Deane
Courtesy of the San Francisco Examiner

Photograph of John P. Dunning
Courtesy of the San Francisco Examiner

Photograph of Mrs. Grace Harris' mother and the defendant, Cordelia Botkin
Courtesy of the San Francisco Examiner

Police Photographs of the Death dealing candy box and it's contents
Courtesy of the San Francisco Call

Bibliography

Books:

Blagg, G. Daniel. *Dover: A Pictorial History.* Virginia Beach: Donning Company, 1980.

de Valinger, Leon, and Virginia Shaw, ed.: *A Calendar of the Ridgely Family Letters 1742 to 1899 in the Delaware State Archives.* Vol. 2. Dover, 1961

Fulton, Cecil C.: *It Happened in Dover 1865 to 1960.* Dover, 1962.

Hancock, Harold: *A History of Kent County Delaware.* Dover: Dover Litho Publishing, 1976.

Jackson, Joseph H., ed.: *San Francisco Murders.* New York: Dual, Sloan, and Pearce, 1947.

Sammik, Emil, and Don 0. Winslow.: *Dover. The First Two Hundred and Fifty Years.* Dover, 1967.

Scharf, J. Thomas.: *History of Delaware 1609 to 1888 (3 volumes).* Westminster: Family Line Publications, 1976.

Lewis Alfred Allen: *The Evidence Never Lies.* With Herbert Leon MacDonell. New York: Holt, Rinehart, and Winstorn, 1984.

Court Decisions:

Cordelia Botkin v. California, Criminal Case No. 632, (1900).

Periodicals:

The Bulletin, San Francisco, California 23 December-31 December, 1898.

The Call, San Francisco, California, 20 August-31 December, 1898; 16 March-13 April, 1904.

Delaware Gazette and State Journal 12 August, 1898-19 January, 1899.

Every Evening, Wilmington, Delaware 12 August-31 December, 1898; 15 March-8 April, 1904.

The Morning News, Wilmington, Delaware 11 March - 8 April, 1904

New York Daily Tribune 31 December, 1898.

Philadelphia Evening Bulletin 16 December, 1898 - 4 January 1899.

San Francisco Chronicle 10 March - 21 April, 1904; 8 March, 1910.
San Francisco Examiner 16 August - 31 December, 1898; 17 March - 12 April, 1904; 8 March 1910.